A Great Success

Mrs Humphry Ward

ESPRIOS DIGITAL PUBLISHING

A Great Success

By

Mrs. Humphry Ward Author of "Eltham House, " "Delia Blanchflower, " etc.

New York Hearst's International Library Co. 1916

PART I

CHAPTER I

"Arthur, —what did you give the man?"

"Half a crown, my dear! Now don't make a fuss. I know exactly what you're going to say!"

"*Half a crown!*" said Doris Meadows, in consternation. "The fare was one and twopence. Of course he thought you mad. But I'll get it back!"

And she ran to the open window, crying "Hi!" to the driver of a taxi-cab, who, having put down his fares, was just on the point of starting from the door of the small semi-detached house in a South Kensington street, which owned Arthur and Doris Meadows for its master and mistress.

The driver turned at her call.

"Hi! —Stop! You've been over-paid!"

The man grinned all over, made her a low bow, and made off as fast as he could.

Arthur Meadows, behind her, went into a fit of laughter, and as his wife, discomfited, turned back into the room he threw a triumphant arm around her.

"I had to give him half a crown, dear, or burst. Just look at these letters—and you know what a post we had this morning! Now don't bother about the taxi! What does it matter? Come and open the post."

Whereupon Doris Meadows felt herself forcibly drawn down to a seat on the sofa beside her husband, who threw a bundle of letters upon his wife's lap, and then turned eagerly to open others with which his own hands were full.

"H'm! —Two more publishers' letters, asking for the book—don't they wish they may get it! But I could have made a far better bargain

A Great Success

if I'd only waited a fortnight. Just my luck! One—two—four—autograph fiends! The last—a lady, of course! —wants a page of the first lecture. Calm! Invitations from the Scottish Athenaeum—the Newcastle Academy—the Birmingham Literary Guild—the Glasgow Poetic Society—the 'British Philosophers'—the Dublin Dilettanti! —Heavens! —how many more! None of them offering cash, as far as I can see—only fame—pure and undefiled! Hullo! —that's a compliment! —the Parnassians have put me on their Council. And last year, I was told, I couldn't even get in as an ordinary member. Dash their impudence!... This is really astounding! What are yours, darling?"

And tumbling all his opened letters on the sofa, Arthur Meadows rose—in sheer excitement—and confronted his wife, with a flushed countenance. He was a tall, broadly built, loose-limbed fellow, with a fine shaggy head, whereof various black locks were apt to fall forward over his eyes, needing to be constantly thrown back by a picturesque action of the hand. The features were large and regular, the complexion dark, the eyes a pale blue, under bushy brows. The whole aspect of the man, indeed, was not unworthy of the adjective "Olympian," already freely applied to it by some of the enthusiastic women students attending his now famous lectures. One girl artist learned in classical archaeology, and a haunter of the British Museum, had made a charcoal study of a well-known archaistic "Diespiter" of the Augustan period, on the same sheet with a rapid sketch of Meadows when lecturing; a performance which had been much handed about in the lecture-room, though always just avoiding—strangely enough—the eyes of the lecturer.
expression of slumbrous power, the mingling of dream and energy in the Olympian countenance, had been, in the opinion of the majority, extremely well caught. Only Doris Meadows, the lecturer's wife, herself an artist, and a much better one than the author of the drawing, had smiled a little queerly on being allowed a sight of it.

However, she was no less excited by the batch of letters her husband had allowed her to open than he by his. Her bundle included, so it appeared, letters from several leading politicians: one, discussing in a most animated and friendly tone the lecture of the week before, on "Lord George Bentinck"; and two others dealing with the first lecture of the series, the brilliant pen-portrait of Disraeli, which—partly owing to feminine influence behind the scenes—had been given *verbatim* and with much preliminary trumpeting in two or three Tory newspapers, and had produced a real sensation, of that mild sort which alone the British public—that does not love lectures—is capable of receiving from the report of one. Persons in the political world had relished its plain speaking; dames and counsellors of the Primrose League had read the praise with avidity, and skipped the criticism; while the mere men and women of letters had appreciated a style crisp, unhackneyed, and alive. The second lecture on "Lord George Bentinck" had been crowded, and the crowd had included several Cabinet Ministers, and those great ladies of the moment who gather like vultures to the feast on any similar occasion. The third lecture, on "Palmerston and Lord John"—had been not only crowded, but crowded out, and London was by now fully aware that it possessed in Arthur Meadows a person capable of painting a series of La Bruyère-like portraits of modern men, as vivid, biting, and "topical"—*mutatis mutandis*—as the great French series were in their day.

Applications for the coming lecture on "Lord Randolph" were arriving by every post, and those to follow after—on men just dead, and others still alive—would probably have to be given in a much larger hall than that at present engaged, so certain was intelligent London that in going to hear Arthur Meadows on the most admired—or the most detested—personalities of the day, they at least ran no risk of wishy-washy panegyric, or a dull caution. Meadows had proved himself daring both in compliment and attack; nothing could be sharper than his thrusts, or more Olympian than his homage. There were those indeed who talked of "airs" and "mannerisms, " but their faint voices were lost in the general shouting.

"Wonderful! " said Doris, at last, looking up from the last of these epistles. "I really didn't know, Arthur, you were such a great man. "

Her eyes rested on him with a fond but rather puzzled expression.

"Well, of course, dear, you've always seen the seamy side of me, " said Meadows, with the slightest change of tone and a laugh. "Perhaps now you'll believe me when I say that I'm not always lazy when I seem so—that a man must have time to think, and smoke, and dawdle, if he's to write anything decent, and can't always rush at the first job that offers. When you thought I was idling—I wasn't! I was gathering up impressions. Then came an attractive piece of work—one that suited me—and I rose to it. There, you see! "

A Great Success

He threw back his Jovian head, with a look at his wife, half combative, half merry.

Doris's forehead puckered a little.

"Well, thank Heaven that it *has* turned out well! " she said, with a deep breath. "Where we should have been if it hadn't I'm sure I don't know! And, as it is—By the way, Arthur, have you got that packet ready for New York? " Her tone was quick and anxious.

"What, the proofs of 'Dizzy'? Oh, goodness, that'll do any time. Don't bother, Doris. I'm really rather done—and this post is—well, upon my word, it's overwhelming! " And, gathering up the letters, he threw himself with an air of fatigue into a long chair, his hands behind his head. "Perhaps after tea and a cigarette I shall feel more fit. "

"Arthur! —you know to-morrow is the last day for catching the New York mail. "

"Well, hang it, if I don't catch it, they must wait, that's all! " said Meadows peevishly. "If they won't take it, somebody else will. "

"They" represented the editor and publisher of a famous New York magazine, who had agreed by cable to give a large sum for the "Dizzy" lecture, provided it reached them by a certain date.

Doris twisted her lip.

"Arthur, *do* think of the bills! "

"Darling, don't be a nuisance! If I succeed I shall make money. And if this isn't a success I don't know what is. " He pointed to the letters on his lap, an impatient gesture which dislodged a certain number of them, so that they came rustling to the floor.

"Hullo! —here's one you haven't opened. Another coronet! Gracious! I believe it's the woman who asked us to dinner a fortnight ago, and we couldn't go. "

Meadows sat up with a jerk, all languor dispelled, and held out his hand for the letter.

"Lady Dunstable! By George! I thought she'd ask us, —though you don't deserve it, Doris, for you didn't take any trouble at all about her first invitation—"

"We were *engaged*!" cried Doris, interrupting him, her eyebrows mounting.

"We could have got out of it perfectly. But now, listen to this:

"Dear Mr. Meadows, —I hope your wife will excuse my writing to you instead of to her, as you and I are already acquainted. Can I induce you both to come to Crosby Ledgers for a week-end, on July 16? We hope to have a pleasant party, a diplomat or two, the Home Secretary, and General Hichen—perhaps some others. You would, I am sure, admire our hill country, and I should like to show you some of the precious autographs we have inherited.

"Yours sincerely,
"RACHEL DUNSTABLE.

"If your wife brings a maid, perhaps she will kindly let me know."

Doris laughed, and the amused scorn of her laugh annoyed her husband. However, at that moment their small house-parlourmaid entered with the tea-tray, and Doris rose to make a place for it. The parlourmaid put it down with much unnecessary noise, and Doris, looking at her in alarm, saw that her expression was sulky and her eyes red. When the girl had departed, Mrs. Meadows said with resignation—

"There! that one will give me notice to-morrow!"

"Well, I'm sure you could easily get a better!" said her husband sharply.

Doris shook her head.

"The fourth in six months!" she said, sighing. "And she really is a good girl."

"I suppose, as usual, she complains of me!" The voice was that of an injured man.

"Yes, dear, she does! They all do. You give them a lot of extra work already, and all these things you have been buying lately—oh, Arthur, if you *wouldn't* buy things! —mean more work. You know that copper coal-scuttle you sent in yesterday? "

"Well, isn't it a beauty? —a real Georgian piece! " cried Meadows, indignantly.

"I dare say it is. But it has to be cleaned. When it arrived Jane came to see me in this room, shut the door, and put her back against it 'There's another of them beastly copper coal-scuttles come! ' You should have seen her eyes blazing. 'And I should like to know, ma'am, who's going to clean it—'cos I can't. ' And I just had to promise her it might go dirty. "

"Lazy minx! " said Meadows, good-humouredly, with his mouth full of tea-cake. "At last I have something good to look at in this room. " He turned his eyes caressingly towards the new coal-scuttle. "I suppose I shall have to clean it myself! "

Doris laughed again—this time almost hysterically—but was checked by a fresh entrance of Jane, who, with an air of defiance, deposited a heavy parcel on a chair beside her mistress, and flounced out again.

"What is this? " said Doris in consternation. "*Books*? More books? Heavens, Arthur, what have you been ordering now! I couldn't sleep last night for thinking of the book-bills. "

"You little goose! Of course, I must buy books! Aren't they my tools, my stock-in-trade? Haven't these lectures justified the book-bills a dozen times over? "

This time Arthur Meadows surveyed his wife in real irritation and disgust.

"But, Arthur! —you could get them *all* at the London Library—you know you could! "

"And pray how much time do I waste in going backwards and forwards after books? Any man of letters worth his salt wants a library of his own—within reach of his hand. "

"Yes, if he can pay for it! " said Doris, with plaintive emphasis, as she ruefully turned over the costly volumes which the parcel contained.

"Don't fash yourself, my dear child! Why, what I'm getting for the Dizzy lecture is alone nearly enough to pay all the book bills. "
"It isn't! And just think of all the others! Well—never mind! "

Doris's protesting mood suddenly collapsed. She sat down on a stool beside her husband, rested her elbow on his knee, and, chin in hand, surveyed him with a softened countenance. Doris Meadows was not a beauty; only pleasant-faced, with good eyes, and a strong, expressive mouth. Her brown hair was perhaps her chief point, and she wore it rippled and coiled so as to set off a shapely head and neck. It was always a secret grievance with her that she had so little positive beauty. And her husband had never flattered her on the subject. In the early days of their marriage she had timidly asked him, after one of their bridal dinner-parties in which she had worn her wedding-dress—"Did I look nice to-night? Do you—do you ever think I look pretty, Arthur? " And he had looked her over, with an odd change of expression—careless affection passing into something critical and cool: —"I'm never ashamed of you, Doris, in any company. Won't you be satisfied with that? " She had been far from satisfied; the phrase had burnt in her memory from then till now. But she knew Arthur had not meant to hurt her, and she bore him no grudge. And, by now, she was too well acquainted with the rubs and prose of life, too much occupied with house-books, and rough servants, and the terror of an overdrawn account, to have any time or thought to spare to her own looks. Fortunately she had an instinctive love for neatness and delicacy; so that her little figure, besides being agile and vigorous—capable of much dignity too on occasion—was of a singular trimness and grace in all its simple appointments. Her trousseau was long since exhausted, and she rarely had a new dress. But slovenly she could not be.

It was the matter of a new dress which was now indeed running in her mind. She took up Lady Dunstable's letter, and read it pensively through again.

"You can accept for yourself, Arthur, of course, " she said, looking up. "But I can't possibly go. "

Meadows protested loudly.

"You have no excuse at all!" he declared hotly. "Lady Dunstable has given us a month's notice. You *can't* get out of it. Do you want me to be known as a man who accepts smart invitations without his wife? There is no more caddish creature in the world."

Doris could not help smiling upon him. But her mouth was none the less determined.

"I haven't got a single frock that's fit for Crosby Ledgers. And I'm not going on tick for a new one!"

"I never heard anything so absurd! Shan't we have more money in a few weeks than we've had for years?"

"I dare say. It's all wanted. Besides, I have my work to finish."

"My dear Doris!"

A slight red mounted in Doris's cheeks.

"Oh, you may be as scornful as you like! But ten pounds is ten pounds, and I like keeping engagements."

The "work" in question meant illustrations for a children's book. Doris had accepted the commission with eagerness, and had been going regularly to the Campden Hill studio of an Academician—her mother's brother—who was glad to supply her with some of the "properties" she wanted for her drawings.

"I shall soon not allow you to do anything of the kind," said Meadows with decision.

"On the contrary! I shall always take paid work when I can get it," was the firm reply—"unless—"

"Unless what?"

"You know," she said quietly. Meadows was silent a moment, then reached out for her hand, which she gave him. They had no children; and, as he well knew, Doris pined for them. The look in her eyes when she nursed her friends' babies had often hurt him. But after all, why despair? It was only four years from their wedding day.

But he was not going to be beaten in the matter of Crosby Ledgers. They had a long and heated discussion, at the end of which Doris surrendered.

"Very well! I shall have to spend a week in doing up my old black gown, and it will be a botch at the end of it. But—*nothing—will induce me*—to get a new one! "

She delivered this ultimatum with her hands behind her, a defeated, but still resolute young person. Meadows, having won the main battle, left the rest to Providence, and went off to his "den" to read all his letters through once more—agreeable task! —and to write a note of acceptance to the Home Secretary, who had asked him to luncheon. Doris was not included in the invitation. "But anybody may ask a husband—or a wife—to lunch, separately. That's understood. I shan't do it often, however—that I can tell them! " And justified by this Spartan temper as to the future, he wrote a charming note, accepting the delights of the present, so full of epigram that the Cabinet Minister to whom it was addressed had no sooner read it than he consigned it instanter to his wife's collection of autographs.

Meanwhile Doris was occupied partly in soothing the injured feelings of Jane, and partly in smoothing out and inspecting her one evening frock. She decided that it would take her a week to "do it up, " and that she would do it herself. "A week wasted! " she thought—"and all for nothing. What do we want with Lady Dunstable! She'll flatter Arthur, and make him lazy. They all do! And I've no use for her at all. *Maid* indeed! Does she think nobody can exist without that appendage? How I should like to make her live on four hundred a year, with a husband that will spend seven! "

She stood, half amused, half frowning, beside the bed on which lay her one evening frock. But the frown passed away, effaced by an expression much softer and tenderer than anything she had allowed Arthur to see of late. Of course she delighted in Arthur's success; she was proud, indeed, through and through. Hadn't she always known that he had this gift, this quick, vivacious power of narrative, this genius—for it was something like it—for literary portraiture? And now at last the stimulus had come—and the opportunity with it. Could she ever forget the anxiety of the first lecture—the difficulty she had had in making him finish it—his careless, unbusiness-like management of the whole affair? But then had come the burst of praise and popularity; and Arthur was a new man. No difficulty—or scarcely—in getting him to work since then! Applause, so new and intoxicating, had lured him on, as she had been wont to lure the black pony of her childhood with a handful of sugar. Yes, her Arthur was a genius; she had always known it. And something of a child too—lazy, wilful, and sensuous—that, too, she had known for some time. And she loved him with all her heart.

"But I won't have him spoilt by those fine ladies! " she said to herself, with frowning clear-sightedness. "They make a perfect fool of him. Now, then, I'd better write to Lady Dunstable. Of course she ought to have written to me! "

So she sat down and wrote:

Dear Lady Dunstable, —We have much pleasure in accepting your kind invitation, and I will let you know our train later. I have no maid, so—

But at this point Mrs. Meadows, struck by a sudden idea, threw down her pen.

"Heavens! —suppose I took Jane? Somebody told me the other day that nobody got any attention at Crosby Ledgers without a maid. And it might bribe Jane into staying. I should feel a horrid snob—but it would be rather fun—especially as Lady Dunstable will certainly be immensely surprised. The fare would be only about five shillings—Jane would get her food for two days at the Dunstables' expense—and I should have a friend. I'll do it. "

So, with her eyes dancing, Doris tore up her note, and began again:

Dear Lady Dunstable, —We have much pleasure in accepting your kind invitation, and I will let you know our train later. As you kindly permit me, I will bring a maid.

        Yours sincerely,
        DORIS MEADOWS.

*****

The month which elapsed between Lady Dunstable's invitation and the Crosby Ledgers party was spent by Doris first in "doing up" her frock, and then in taking the bloom off it at various dinner-parties to which they were already invited as the "celebrities" of the moment; in making Arthur's wardrobe presentable; in watching over the tickets and receipts of the weekly lectures; in collecting the press cuttings about them; in finishing her illustrations; and in instructing the awe-struck Jane, now perfectly amenable, in the mysteries that would be expected of her.

Meanwhile Mrs. Meadows heard various accounts from artistic and literary friends of the parties at Crosby Ledgers. These accounts were generally prefaced by the laughing remark, "But anything *I* can say is ancient history. Lady Dunstable dropped us long ago!"

Anyway, it appeared that the mistress of Crosby Ledgers could be charming, and could also be exactly the reverse. She was a creature of whims and did precisely as she pleased. Everything she did apparently was acceptable to Lord Dunstable, who admired her blindly. But in one point at least she was a disappointed woman. Her son, an unsatisfactory youth of two-and-twenty, was seldom to be seen under his parents' roof, and it was rumoured that he had already given them a great deal of trouble.

"The dreadful thing, my dear, is the *games* they play!" said the wife of a dramatist, whose one successful piece had been followed by years of ill-fortune.

"*Games?*" said Doris. "Do you mean cards—for money?"

"Oh, dear no! Intellectual games. *Bouts-rimés;* translations—Lady Dunstable looks out the bits and some people think the words—beforehand; paragraphs on a subject—in a particular style—Pater's, or Ruskin's, or Carlyle's. Each person throws two slips into a hat. On one you write the subject, on another the name of the author whose style is to be imitated. Then you draw. Of course Lady Dunstable carries off all the honours. But then everybody believes she spends all the mornings preparing these things. She never comes down till nearly lunch."

"This is really appalling!" said Doris, with round eyes. "I have forgotten everything I ever knew."

As for her own impressions of the great lady, she had only seen her once in the semi-darkness of the lecture-room, and could only remember a long, sallow face, with striking black eyes and a pointed chin, a general look of distinction and an air of one accustomed to the "chief seat" at any board—whether the feasts of reason or those of a more ordinary kind.

As the days went on, Doris, for all her sturdy self-reliance, began to feel a little nervous inwardly. She had been quite well-educated, first at a good High School, and then in the class-rooms of a provincial University; and, as the clever daughter of a clever doctor in large practice, she had always been in touch with the intellectual world, especially on its scientific side. And for nearly two years before her marriage she had been a student at the Slade School. But since her imprudent love-match with a literary man had plunged her into the practical work of a small household, run on a scanty and precarious income, she had been obliged, one after another, to let the old interests go. Except the drawing. That was good enough to bring her a little money, as an illustrator, designer of Christmas cards, etc. ; and she filled most of her spare time with it.

But now she feverishly looked out some of her old books—Pater's "Studies, " a volume of Huxley's Essays, "Shelley" and "Keats" in the "Men of Letters" series. She borrowed two or three of the political biographies with which Arthur's shelves were crowded, having all the while, however, the dispiriting conviction that Lady Dunstable had been dandled on the knees of every English Prime Minister since her birth, and had been the blood relation of all of them, except perhaps Mr. G., whose blood no doubt had not been blue enough to entitle him to the privilege.

However, she must do her best. She kept these feelings and preparations entirely secret from Arthur, and she saw the day of the visit dawn in a mood of mingled expectation and revolt.

CHAPTER II

It was a perfect June evening: Doris was seated on one of the spreading lawns of Crosby Ledgers, —a low Georgian house, much added to at various times, and now a pleasant medley of pillared verandahs, tiled roofs, cupolas, and dormer windows, apparently unpretending, but, as many people knew, one of the most luxurious of English country houses.

Lady Dunstable, in a flowing dress of lilac crêpe and a large black hat, had just given Mrs. Meadows a second cup of tea, and was clearly doing her duty—and showing it—to a guest whose entertainment could not be trusted to go of itself. The only other persons at the tea-table—the Meadowses having arrived late—were an elderly man with long Dundreary whiskers, in a Panama hat and a white waistcoat, and a lady of uncertain age, plump, kind-eyed, and merry-mouthed, in whom Doris had at once divined a possible harbour of refuge from the terrors of the situation. Arthur was strolling up and down the lawn with the Home Secretary, smoking and chatting—talking indeed nineteen to the dozen, and entirely at his ease. A few other groups were scattered over the grass; while girls in white dresses and young men in flannels were playing tennis in the distance. A lake at the bottom of the sloping garden made light and space in a landscape otherwise too heavily walled in by thick woodland. White swans floated on the lake, and the June trees beyond were in their freshest and proudest leaf. A church tower rose appropriately in a corner of the park, and on the other side of the deer-fence beyond the lake a herd of red deer were feeding. Doris could not help feeling as though the whole scene had been lately painted for a new "high life" play at the St. James's Theatre, and she half expected to see Sir George Alexander walk out of the bushes.

"I suppose, Mrs. Meadows, you have been helping your husband with his lectures? " said Lady Dunstable, a little languidly, as though the heat oppressed her. She was making play with a cigarette and her half-shut eyes were fixed on the "lion's" wife. The eyes fascinated Doris. Surely they were artificially blackened, above and below? And the lips—had art been delicately invoked, or was Nature alone responsible?

"I copy things for Arthur, " said Doris. "Unfortunately, I can't type. "

A Great Success

At the sound of the young and musical voice, the gentleman with the Dundreary whiskers—Sir Luke Malford—who had seemed half asleep, turned sharply to look at the speaker. Doris too was in a white dress, of the simplest stuff and make; but it became her. So did the straw hat, with its wreath of wild roses, which she had trimmed herself that morning. There was not the slightest visible sign of tremor in the young woman; and Sir Luke's inner mind applauded her.

"No fool! —and a lady, " he thought. "Let's see what Rachel will make of her. "

"Then you don't help him in the writing? " said Lady Dunstable, still with the same detached air. Doris laughed.

"I don't know what Arthur would say if I proposed it. He never lets anybody go near him when he's writing. "

"I see; like all geniuses, he's dangerous on the loose. " Was Lady Dunstable's smile just touched with sarcasm? "Well! —has the success of the lectures surprised you? "

Doris pondered.

"No, " she said at last, "not really. I always thought Arthur had it in him. "

"But you hardly expected such a run—such an excitement! "

"I don't know, " said Doris, coolly. "I think I did—sometimes. The question is how long it will last. "

She looked, smiling, at her interrogator.

The gentleman with the whiskers stooped across the table.

"Oh, nothing lasts in this world. But that of course is what makes a good time so good. "

Doris turned towards him—demurring—for the sake of conversation. "I never could understand how Cinderella enjoyed the ball. "

"For thinking of the clock?" laughed Sir Luke. "No, no! —you can't mean that. It's the expectation of the clock that doubles the pleasure. Of course you agree, Rachel!"—he turned to her—"else why did you read me that very doleful poem yesterday, on this very theme? — that it's only the certainty of death that makes life agreeable? By the way, George Eliot had said it before!"

"The poem was by a friend of mine," said Lady Dunstable, coldly. "I read it to you to see how it sounded. But I thought it poor stuff."

"How unkind of you! The man who wrote it says he lives upon your friendship."

"That, perhaps, is why he's so thin."

Sir Luke laughed again.

"To be sure, I saw the poor man—after you had talked to him the other night—going to Dunstable to be consoled. Poor George! he's always healing the wounds you make."

"Of course. That's why I married him. George says all the civil things. That sets me free to do the rude ones."

"Rachel!" The exclamation came from the plump lady opposite, who was smiling broadly, and showing some very white teeth. A signal passed from her eyes to those of Doris, as though to say "Don't be alarmed!"

But Doris was not at all alarmed. She was eagerly watching Lady Dunstable, as one watches for the mannerisms of some well-known performer. Sir Luke perceived it, and immediately began to show off his hostess by one of the sparring matches that were apparently frequent between them. They fell to discussing a party of guests—landowners from a neighbouring estate—who seemed to have paid a visit to Crosby Ledgers the day before. Lady Dunstable had not enjoyed them, and her tongue on the subject was sharpness itself, restrained by none of the ordinary compunctions. "Is this how she talks about all her guests—on Monday morning?" thought Doris, with quickened pulse as the biting sentences flew about.

... "Mr. Worthing? Why did he marry her? Oh, because he wanted a stuffed goose to sit by the fire while he went out and amused himself.... Why did she marry him? Ah, that's more difficult to answer. Is one obliged to credit Mrs. Worthing with any reasons—on any subject? However, I like Mr. Worthing—he's what men ought to be."

"And that is—?" Doris ventured to put in.

"Just—men," said Lady Dunstable, shortly.

Sir Luke laughed over his cigarette.

"That you may fool them? Well, Rachel, all the same, you would die of Worthing's company in a month."

"I shouldn't die," said Lady Dunstable, quietly. "I should murder."

"Hullo, what's my wife talking about?" said a bluff and friendly voice. Doris looked up to see a handsome man with grizzled hair approaching.

"Mrs. Meadows? How do you do? What a beautiful evening you've brought! Your husband and I have been having a jolly talk. My word! —he's a clever chap. Let me congratulate you on the lectures. Biggest success known in recent days!"

Doris beamed upon her host, well pleased, and he settled down beside her, doing his kind best to entertain her. In him, all those protective feelings towards a stranger, in which his wife appeared to be conspicuously lacking, were to be discerned on first acquaintance. Doris was practically sure that his inner mind was thinking—"Poor little thing! —knows nobody here. Rachel's been scaring her. Must look after her!"

And look after her he did. He was by no means an amusing companion. Lazy, gentle, and ineffective, Doris quickly perceived that he was entirely eclipsed by his wife, who, now that she was relieved of Mrs. Meadows, was soon surrounded by a congenial company—the Home Secretary, one or two other politicians, the old General, a literary Dean, Lord Staines, a great racing man, Arthur Meadows, and one or two more. The talk became almost entirely political—with a dash of literature. Doris saw at once that Lady Dunstable was the centre of it, and she was not long in guessing that it was for this kind of talk that people came to Crosby Ledgers. Lady

A Great Success

Dunstable, it seemed, was capable of talking like a man with men, and like a man of affairs with the men of affairs. Her political knowledge was astonishing; so, evidently, was her background of family and tradition, interwoven throughout with English political history. English statesmen had not only dandled her, they had taught her, walked with her, written to her, and—no doubt—flirted with her. Doris, as she listened to her, disliked her heartily, and at the same time could not help being thrilled by so much knowledge, so much contact with history in the making, and by such a masterful way, in a woman, with the great ones of the earth. "What a worm she must think me!" thought Doris—"what a worm she *does* think me—and the likes of me!"

At the same time, the spectator must needs admit there was something else in Lady Dunstable's talk than mere intelligence or mere mannishness. There was undoubtedly something of "the good fellow," and, through all her hard hitting, a curious absence—in conversation—of the personal egotism she was quite ready to show in all the trifles of life. On the present occasion her main object clearly was to bring out Arthur Meadows—the new captive of her bow and spear; to find out what was in him; to see if he was worthy of her inner circle. Throwing all compliment aside, she attacked him hotly on certain statements—certain estimates—in his lectures. Her knowledge was personal; the knowledge of one whose father had sat in Dizzy's latest Cabinet, while, through the endless cousinship of the English landed families, she was as much related to the Whig as to the Tory leaders of the past. She talked familiarly of "Uncle This" or "Cousin That," who had been apparently the idols of her nursery before they had become the heroes of England; and Meadows had much ado to defend himself against her store of anecdote and reminiscence. "Unfair!" thought Doris, breathlessly watching the contest of wits. "Oh, if she weren't a woman, Arthur could easily beat her!"

But she was a woman, and not at all unwilling, when hard pressed, to take advantage of that fact.

All the same, Meadows was stirred to most unwonted efforts. He proved to be an antagonist worth her steel; and Doris's heart swelled with secret pride as she saw how all the other voices died down, how more and more people came up to listen, even the young men and maidens,—throwing themselves on the grass, around the two disputants. Finally Lady Dunstable carried off the honours. Had she not seen Lord Beaconsfield twice during the fatal week of his last general election, when England turned against him, when his great rival triumphed, and all was lost? Had he not talked to her, as great men will talk to the young and charming women whose flatteries soften their defeats; so that, from the wings, she had seen almost the last of that well-graced actor, caught his last gestures and some of his last words?

"Brava, brava! " said Meadows, when the story ceased, although it had been intended to upset one of his own most brilliant generalisations; and a sound of clapping hands went round the circle. Lady Dunstable, a little flushed and panting, smiled and was silent. Meadows, meanwhile, was thinking—"How often has she told that tale? She has it by heart. Every touch in it has been sharpened a dozen times. All the same—a wonderful performance!"

Lord Dunstable, meanwhile, sat absolutely silent, his hat on the back of his head, his attention fixed on his wife. As the group broke up, and the chairs were pushed back, he said in Doris's ear—"Isn't she an awfully clever woman, my wife? "

Before Doris could answer, she heard Lady Dunstable carelessly—but none the less peremptorily—inviting her women guests to see their rooms. Doris walked by her hostess's side towards the house. Every trace of animation and charm had now vanished from that lady's manner. She was as languid and monosyllabic as before, and Doris could only feel once again that while her clever husband was an eagerly welcomed guest, she herself could only expect to reckon as his appendage—a piece of family luggage.

Lady Dunstable threw open the door of a spacious bedroom. "No doubt you will wish to rest till dinner, " she said, severely. "And of course your maid will ask for what she wants. " At the word "maid, " did Doris dream it, or was there a satiric gleam in the hard black eyes? "Pretender, " it seemed to say—and Doris's conscience admitted the charge.

And indeed the door had no sooner closed on Lady Dunstable before an agitated knock announced Jane—in tears.

She stood opposite her mistress in desperation.

A Great Success

"Please, ma'am—I'll have to have an evening dress—or I can't go in to supper!"

"What on earth do you mean?" said Doris, staring at her.

"Every maid in this 'ouse, ma'am, 'as got to dress for supper. The maids go in the 'ousekeeper's room, an' they've all on 'em got dresses V-shaped, or cut square, or something. This black dress, ma'am, won't do at all. So I can't have no supper. I couldn't dream, ma'am, of goin' in different to the others!"

"You silly creature!" said Doris, springing up. "Look here—I'll lend you my spare blouse. You can turn it in at the neck, and wear my white scarf. You'll be as smart as any of them!"

And half laughing, half compassionate, she pulled her blouse out of the box, adjusted the white scarf to it herself, and sent the bewildered Jane about her business, after having shown her first how to unpack her mistress's modest belongings, and strictly charged her to return half an hour before dinner. "Of course I shall dress myself,—but you may as well have a lesson."

The girl went, and Doris was left stormily wondering why she had been such a fool as to bring her. Then her sense of humour conquered, and her brow cleared. She went to the open window and stood looking over the park beyond. Sunset lay broad and rich over the wide stretches of grass, and on the splendid oaks lifting their dazzling leaf to the purest of skies. The roses in the garden sent up their scent, there was a plashing of water from an invisible fountain, and the deer beyond the fence wandered in and out of the broad bands of shadow drawn across the park. Doris's young feet fidgeted under her. She longed to be out exploring the woods and the lake. Why was she immured in this stupid room, to which Lady Dunstable had conducted her with a chill politeness which had said plainly enough "Here you are—and here you stay!—till dinner!"

"If I could only find a back-staircase," she thought, "I would soon be enjoying myself! Arthur, lucky wretch, said something about playing golf. No!—there he is!"

And sure enough, on the farthest edge of the lawn going towards the park, she saw two figures walking—Lady Dunstable and Arthur! "Deep in talk of course—having the best of times—while I am shut up here—half-past six! —on a glorious evening! " The reflection, however, was, on the whole, good-humoured. She did not feel, as yet, either jealous or tragic. Some day, she supposed, if it was to be her lot to visit country houses, she would get used to their ways. For Arthur, of course, it was useful—perhaps necessary—to be put through his paces by a woman like Lady Dunstable. "And he can hold his own. But for me? I contribute nothing. I don't belong to them—they don't want me—and what use have I for them? "

Her meditations, however, were here interrupted by a knock. On her saying "Come in"—the door opened cautiously to admit the face of the substantial lady, Miss Field, to whom Doris had been introduced at the tea-table.

"Are you resting? " said Miss Field, "or only 'interned'? "

"Oh, please come in! " cried Doris. "I never was less tired in my life. "

Miss Field entered, and took the armchair that Doris offered her, fronting the open window and the summer scene. Her face would have suited the Muse of Mirth, if any Muse is ever forty years of age. The small, up-turned nose and full red lips were always smiling; so were the eyes; and the fair skin and still golden hair, the plump figure and gay dress of flower-sprigged muslin, were all in keeping with the part.

"You have never seen my cousin before? " she inquired.

"Lady Dunstable? Is she your cousin? "

Miss Field nodded. "My first cousin. And I spend a great part of the year here, helping in different ways. Rachel can't do without me now, so I'm able to keep her in order. Don't ever be shy with her! Don't ever let her think she frightens you! —those are the two indispensable rules here. "

"I'm afraid I should break them, " said Doris, slowly. "She does frighten me—horribly! "

"Ah, well, you didn't show it—that's the chief thing. You know she's a much more human creature than she seems. "

"Is she? " Doris's eyes pursued the two distant figures in the park.

A Great Success

"You'd think, for instance, that Lord Dunstable was just a cipher? Not at all. He's the real authority here, and when he puts his foot down Rachel always gives in. But of course she's stood in the way of his career."

Doris shrank a little from these indiscretions. But she could not keep her curiosity out of her eyes, and Miss Field smilingly answered it.

"She's absorbed him so! You see he watches her all the time. She's like an endless play to him. He really doesn't care for anything else—he doesn't want anything else. Of course they're very rich. But he might have done something in politics, if she hadn't been so much more important than he. And then, naturally, she's made enemies—powerful enemies. Her friends come here of course—her old cronies—the people who can put up with her. They're devoted to her. And the young people—the very modern ones—who think nice manners 'early Victorian,' and like her rudeness for the sake of her cleverness. But the rest! —What do you think she did at one of these parties last year?"

Doris could not help wishing to know.

"She took a fancy to ask a girl near here—the daughter of a clergyman, a great friend of Lord Dunstable's, to come over for the Sunday. Lord Dunstable had talked of the girl, and Rachel's always on the look-out for cleverness; she hunts it like a hound! She met the young woman too somewhere, and got the impression—I can't say how—that she would 'go.' So on the Saturday morning she went over in her pony-carriage—broke in on the little Rectory like a hurricane—of course you know the people about here regard her as something semi-divine! —and told the girl she had come to take her back to Crosby Ledgers for the Sunday. So the poor child packed up, all in a flutter, and they set off together in the pony-carriage—six miles. And by the time they had gone four Rachel had discovered she had made a mistake—that the girl wasn't clever, and would add nothing to the party. So she quietly told her that she was afraid, after all, the party wouldn't suit her. And then she turned the pony's head, and drove her straight home again!"

"Oh!" cried Doris, her cheeks red, her eyes aflame.

"Brutal, wasn't it? " said the other. "All the same, there are fine things in Rachel. And in one point she's the most vulnerable of women! "

"Her son? " Doris ventured.

Miss Field shrugged her shoulders.

"He doesn't drink—he doesn't gamble—he doesn't spend money—he doesn't run away with other people's wives. He's just nothing! — just incurably empty and idle. He comes here very little. His mother terrifies him. And since he was twenty-one he has a little money of his own. He hangs about in studios and theatres. His mother doesn't know any of his friends. What she suffers—poor Rachel! She'd have given everything in the world for a brilliant son. But you can't wonder. She's like some strong plant that takes all the nourishment out of the ground, so that the plants near it starve. She can't help it. She doesn't mean to be a vampire! "

Doris hardly knew what to say. Somehow she wished the vampire were not walking with Arthur! That, however, was not a sentiment easily communicable; and she was just turning it into something else when Miss Field said—abruptly, like someone coming to the real point—

"Does your husband like her? "

"Why yes, of course! " stammered Doris. "She's been awfully kind to us about the lectures, and—he loves arguing with her. "

"She loves arguing with *him*! " 'said Miss Field triumphantly. "She lives just for such half-hours as that she gave us on the lawn after tea—and all owing to him—he was so inspiring, so stimulating. Oh, you'll see, she'll take you up tremendously—if you want to be taken up! "

The smiling blue eyes looked gaily into Doris's puzzled countenance. Evidently the speaker was much amused by the Meadowses' situation—more amused than her sense of politeness allowed her to explain. Doris was conscious of a vague resentment.

"I'm afraid I don't see what Lady Dunstable will get out of me, " she said, drily.

A Great Success

Miss Field raised her eyebrows.

"Are you going then to let him come here alone? She'll be always asking you! Oh, you needn't be afraid—" and this most candid of cousins laughed aloud. "Rachel isn't a flirt—except of the intellectual kind. But she takes possession—she sticks like a limpet."

There was a pause. Then Miss Field added:

"You mustn't think it odd that I say these things about Rachel. I have to explain her to people. She's not like anybody else."

Doris did not quite see the necessity, but she kept the reflection to herself, and Miss Field passed lightly to the other guests—Sir Luke, a tame cat of the house, who quarrelled with Lady Dunstable once a month, vowed he would never come near her again, and always reappeared; the Dean, who in return for a general submission, was allowed to scold her occasionally for her soul's health; the politicians whom she could not do without, who were therefore handled more gingerly than the rest; the military and naval men who loved Dunstable and put up with his wife for his sake; and the young people—nephews and nieces and cousins—who liked an unconventional hostess without any foolish notions of chaperonage, and always enjoyed themselves famously at Crosby Ledgers.

"Now then," said Miss Field, rising at last, "I think you have the *carte du pays*—and there they are, coming back." She pointed to Meadows and Lady Dunstable, crossing the lawn. "Whatever you do, hold your own. If you don't want to play games, don't play them. If you want to go to church to-morrow, go to church. Lady Dunstable of course is a heathen. And now perhaps, you might *really* rest."

"Such a jolly walk!" said Meadows, entering his wife's room flushed with exercise and pleasure. "The place is divine, and really Lady Dunstable is uncommonly good talk. Hope you haven't been dull, dear?"

Doris replied, laughing, that Miss Field had taken pity on what would otherwise have been solitary confinement, and that now it was time to dress. Meadows kissed her absently, and, with his head evidently still full of his walk, went to his dressing-room. When he reappeared, it was to find Doris attired in a little black gown, with which he was already too familiar. She saw at once the dissatisfaction in his face.

"I can't help it! " she said, with emphasis. "I did my best with it, Arthur, but I'm not a genius at dressmaking. Never mind. Nobody will take any notice of me. "

He quite crossly rebuked her. She really must spend more on her dress. It was unseemly—absurd. She looked as nice as anybody when she was properly got up.

"Well, don't buy any more copper coal-scuttles! " she said slyly, as she straightened his tie, and dropped a kiss on his chin. "Then we'll see. "

They went down to dinner, and on the staircase Meadows turned to say to his wife in a lowered voice:

"Lady Dunstable wants me to go to them in Scotland—for two or three weeks. I dare say I could do some work. "

"Oh, does she? " said Doris.

* * * * *

What perversity drove Lady Dunstable during the evening and the Sunday that followed to match every attention that was lavished on Arthur Meadows by some slight to his wife, will never be known. But the fact was patent. Throughout the diversions or occupations of the forty-eight hours' visit, Mrs. Meadows was either ignored, snubbed, or contradicted. Only Arthur Meadows, indeed, measuring himself with delight, for the first time, against some of the keenest brains in the country, failed to see it. His blindness allowed Lady Dunstable to run a somewhat dangerous course, unchecked. She risked alienating a man whom she particularly wished to attract; she excited a passion of antagonism in Doris's generally equable breast, and was quite aware of it. Notwithstanding, she followed her whim; and by the Sunday evening there existed between the great lady and her guest a state of veiled war, in which the strokes were by no means always to the advantage of Lady Dunstable.

Doris, for instance, with other guests, expressed a wish to attend morning service on Sunday at a famous cathedral some three miles away. Lady Dunstable immediately announced that everybody who wished to go to church would go to the village church within the park, for which alone carriages would be provided. Then Doris and Sir Luke combined, and walked to the cathedral, three miles there and three miles back—to the huge delight of the other and more docile guests. Sunday evening, again, was devastated by what were called "games" at Crosby Ledgers. "Gad, if I wouldn't sooner go in for the Indian Civil again! " said Sir Luke. Doris, with the most ingratiating manner, but quite firmly, begged to be excused. Lady Dunstable bit her lip, and presently, *à propos de bottes*, launched some observations on the need of co-operation in society. It was shirking—refusing to take a hand, to do one's best—false shame, indeed! —that ruined English society and English talk. Let everybody take a lesson from the French! After which the lists were opened, so to speak, and Lady Dunstable, Meadows, the Dean, and about half the young people produced elegant pieces of translation, astounding copies of impromptu verse, essays in all the leading styles of the day, and riddles by the score. The Home Secretary, who had been lassoed by his hostess, escaped towards the middle of the ordeal, and wandered sadly into a further room where Doris sat chatting with Lord Dunstable. He was carrying various slips of paper in his hand, and asked her distractedly if she could throw any light on the question—"Why is Lord Salisbury like a poker? "

"I can't think of anything to say, " he said helplessly, "except 'because they are both upright. ' And here's another—'Why is the Pope like a thermometer? ' I did see some light on that! " His countenance cheered a little. "Would this do? 'Because both are higher in Italy than in England. ' Not very good! —but I must think of something. "

Doris put her wits to his. Between them they polished the riddle; but by the time it was done the Home Secretary had begun to find Meadows's little wife, whose existence he had not noticed hitherto, more agreeable than Lady Dunstable's table with its racked countenances, and its too ample supply of pencils and paper. A deadly crime! When Lady Dunstable, on the stroke of midnight, swept through the rooms to gather her guests for bed, she cast a withering glance on Doris and her companion.

"So you despised our little amusements? " she said, as she handed Mrs. Meadows her candle.

"I wasn't worthy of them, " smiled Doris, in reply.

*****

"Well, I call that a delightful visit! " said Meadows as the train next morning pulled out of the Crosby Ledgers station for London. "I feel freshened up all over. "

Doris looked at him with rather mocking eyes, but said nothing. She fully recognised, however, that Arthur would have been an ungrateful wretch if he had not enjoyed it. Lady Dunstable had been, so to speak, at his feet, and all her little court had taken their cue from her. He had been flattered, drawn out, and shown off to his heart's content, and had been most naturally and humanly happy. "And I, " thought Doris with sudden repentance, "was just a spiky, horrid little toad! What was wrong with me? " She was still searching, when Meadows said reproachfully:

"I thought, darling, you might have taken a little more trouble to make friends with Lady Dunstable. However, that'll be all right. I told her, of course, we should be delighted to go to Scotland. "

"Arthur! " cried Doris, aghast. "Three weeks! I couldn't, Arthur! Don't ask me! "

"And, pray, why? " he angrily inquired.

"Because—oh, Arthur, don't you understand? She is a man's woman. She took a particular dislike to me, and I just had to be stubborn and thorny to get on at all. I'm awfully sorry—but I *couldn't* stay with her, and I'm certain you wouldn't be happy either. "

"I should be perfectly happy, " said Meadows, with vehemence. "And so would you, if you weren't so critical and censorious. Anyway"—his Jove-like mouth shut firmly—"I have promised. "

"You couldn't promise for me! " cried Doris, holding her head very high.

"Then you'll have to let me go without you? "

"Which, of course, was what you swore not to do! " she said, provokingly. "I thought my wife was a reasonable woman! Lady

Dunstable rouses all my powers; she gives me ideas which may be most valuable. It is to the interest of both of us that I should keep up my friendship with her."

"Then keep it up, " said Doris, her cheeks aflame. "But you won't want me to help you, Arthur."

He cried out that it was only pride and conceit that made her behave so. In her heart of hearts, Doris mostly agreed with him. But she wouldn't confess it, and it was presently understood between them that Meadows would duly accept the Dunstables' invitation for August, and that Doris would stay behind.

After which, Doris looked steadily out of the window for the rest of the journey, and could not at all conceal from herself that she had never felt more miserable in her life. The only person in the trio who returned to the Kensington house entirely happy was Jane, who spent the greater part of the day in describing to Martha, the cook-general, the glories of Crosby Ledgers, and her own genteel appearance in Mrs. Meadows's blouse.

PART II

CHAPTER III

During the weeks that followed the Meadowses' first visit to Crosby Ledgers, Doris's conscience was by no means asleep on the subject of Lady Dunstable. She felt that her behaviour in that lady's house, and the sudden growth in her own mind of a quite unmanageable dislike, were not to be defended in one who prided herself on a general temper of coolness and common sense, who despised the rancour and whims of other women, hated scenes, and had always held jealousy to be the smallest and most degrading of passions. Why not laugh at what was odious, show oneself superior to personal slights, and enjoy what could be enjoyed? And above all, why grudge Arthur a woman friend?

None of these arguments, however, availed at all to reconcile Doris to the new intimacy growing under her eyes. The Dunstables came to town, and invitations followed. Mr. and Mrs. Meadows were asked to a large dinner-party, and Doris held her peace and went. She found herself at the end of a long table with an inarticulate schoolboy of seventeen, a ward of Lord Dunstable's, on her left, and with an elderly colonel on her right, who, after a little cool examination of her through an eyeglass, decided to devote himself to the *débutante* on his other side, a Lady Rosamond, who was ready to chatter hunting and horses to him through the whole of dinner. The girl was not pretty, but she was fresh and gay, and Doris, tired with "much serving," envied her spirits, her evident assumption that the world only existed for her to laugh and ride in, her childish unspoken claim to the best of everything—clothes, food, amusements, lovers. Doris on her side made valiant efforts with the schoolboy. She liked boys, and prided herself on getting on with them. But this specimen had no conversation—at any rate for the female sex—and apparently only an appetite. He ate steadily through the dinner, and seemed rather to resent Doris's attempts to distract him from the task. So that presently Doris found herself reduced to long tracts of silence, when her fan was her only companion, and the watching of other people her only amusement.

Lord and Lady Dunstable faced each other at the sides of the table, which was purposely narrow, so that talk could pass across it. Lady Dunstable sat between an Ambassador and a Cabinet Minister, but

Meadows was almost directly opposite to her, and it seemed to be her chief business to make him the hero of the occasion. It was she who drew him into political or literary discussion with the Cabinet Minister, so that the neighbours of each stayed their own talk to listen; she who would insist on his repeating "that story you told me at Crosby Ledgers; " who attacked him abruptly—rudely even, as she had done in the country—so that he might defend himself; and when he had slipped into all her traps one after the other, would fall back in her chair with a little satisfied smile. Doris, silent and forgotten, could not keep her eyes for long from the two distant figures—from this new Arthur, and the sallow-faced, dark-eyed witch who had waved her wand over him.

Wasn't she glad to see her husband courted—valued as he deserved—borne along the growing stream of fame? What matter, if she could only watch him from the bank? —and if the impetuous stream were carrying him away from her? No! She wasn't glad. Some cold and deadly thing seemed to be twining about her heart. Were they leaving the dear, poverty-stricken, debt-pestered life behind for ever, in which, after all, they had been so happy: she, everything to Arthur, and he, so dependent upon her? No doubt she had been driven to despair, often, by his careless, shiftless ways; she had thirsted for success and money; just money enough, at least, to get along with. And now success had come, and money was coming. And here she was, longing for the old, hard, struggling past—hating the advent of the new and glittering future. As she sat at Lady Dunstable's table, she seemed to see the little room in their Kensington house, with the big hole in the carpet, the piles of papers and books, the reading-lamp that would smoke, her work-basket, the house-books, Arthur pulling contentedly at his pipe, the fire crackling between them, his shabby coat, her shabby dress—Bliss! — compared to this splendid scene, with the great Vandycks looking down on the dinner-table, the crowd of guests and servants, the costly food, the dresses, and the diamonds—with, in the distance, *her* Arthur, divided, as it seemed, from her by a growing chasm, never remembering to throw her a look or a smile, drinking in a tide of flattery he would once have been the first to scorn, captured, exhibited, befooled by an unscrupulous, egotistical woman, who would drop him like a squeezed orange when he had ceased to amuse her. And the worst of it was that the woman was not a mere pretender! She had a fine, hard brain, —"as good as Arthur's— nearly—and he knows it. It is that which attracts him—and excites him. I can mend his socks; I can listen while he reads; and he used to like it when I praised. Now, what I say will never matter to him any more; that was just sentiment and nonsense; now, he only wants to know what *she* says; —that's business! He writes with her in his mind—and when he has finished something he sends it off to her, straight. I may see it when all the world may—but she has the first-fruits!"

And in poor Doris's troubled mind the whole scene—save the two central figures, Lady Dunstable and Arthur—seemed to melt away. She was not the first wife, by a long way, into whose quiet breast Lady Dunstable had dropped these seeds of discord. She knew it well by report; but it was hateful, both to wifely feeling and natural vanity, that *she* should now be the victim of the moment, and should know no more than her predecessors how to defend herself. "Why can't I be cool and cutting—pay her back when she is rude, and contradict her when she's absurd? She *is* absurd often. But I think of the right things to say just five minutes too late. I have no nerve—that's the point! —only *l'esprit d'escalier* to perfection. And she has been trained to this sort of campaigning from her babyhood. No good growling! I shall never hold my own!"

Then, into this despairing mood there dropped suddenly a fragment of her neighbour, the Colonel's, conversation—"Mrs. So-and-so? Impossible woman! Oh, one doesn't mind seeing her graze occasionally at the other end of one's table—as the price of getting her husband, don't you know? —but—"

Doris's sudden laugh at the Colonel's elbow startled that gentleman so that he turned round to look at her. But she was absorbed in the menu, which she had taken up, and he could only suppose that something in it amused her.

A few days later arrived a letter for Meadows, which he handed to his wife in silence. There had been no further discussion of Lady Dunstable between them; only a general sense of friction, warnings of hidden fire on Doris's side, and resentment on his, quite new in their relation to each other. Meadows clearly thought that his wife was behaving very badly. Lady Dunstable's efforts on his behalf had already done him substantial service; she had introduced him to all kinds of people likely to help him, intellectually and financially; and to help him was to help Doris. Why would she be such a little fool? So unlike her, too! —sensible, level-headed creature that she generally was. But he was afraid of losing his own temper, if he argued with her. And indeed his lazy easy-goingness loathed argument of this domestic sort, loathed scenes, loathed doing anything disagreeable that could be put off.

But here was Lady Dunstable's letter:

Dear Mr. Arthur, —Will your wife forgive me if I ask you to come to a tiny *men's* dinner-party next Friday at 8.15—to meet the President of the Duma, and another Russian, an intimate friend of Tolstoy's? All males, but myself! So I hope Mrs. Meadows will let you come.

        Yours sincerely,
        RACHEL DUNSTABLE.

"Of course, I won't go if you don't like it, Doris, " said Meadows with the smile of magnanimity.

"I thought you were angry with me—once—for even suggesting that you might! " Doris's tone was light, but not pleasing to a husband's ears. She was busy at the moment in packing up the American proofs of the Disraeli lecture, which at last with infinite difficulty she had persuaded Meadows to correct and return.

"Well—but of course—this is exceptional! " said Meadows, pacing up and down irresolutely.

"Everything's exceptional—in that quarter, " said Doris, in the same tone. "Oh, go, of course! —it would be a thousand pities not to go. "

Meadows at once took her at her word. That was the first of a series of "male" dinners, to which, however, it seemed to Doris, if one might judge from Arthur's accounts, that a good many female exceptions were admitted, no doubt by way of proving the rule. And during July, Meadows lunched in town—in the lofty regions of St. James's or Mayfair—with other enthusiastic women admirers, most of them endowed with long purses and long pedigrees, at least three or four times a week. Doris was occasionally asked and sometimes went. But she was suffering all the time from an initial discouragement and depression, which took away self-reliance, and left her awkwardly conscious. She struggled, but in vain. The world into which Arthur was being so suddenly swept was strange to her, and in many ways antipathetic; but had she been happy and in spirits she could have grappled with it, or rather she could have lost herself in Arthur's success. Had she not always been his slave? But she was not happy! In their obscure days she had been Arthur's best friend, as well as his wife. And it was the old comradeship which was failing her; encroached upon, filched from her, by other women; and especially by this exacting, absorbing woman, whose craze for Arthur Meadows's society was rapidly becoming an amusement and a scandal even to those well acquainted with her previous records of the same sort.

*****

The end of July arrived. The Dunstables left town. At a concert, for which she had herself sent them tickets, Lady Dunstable met Doris and her husband, the night before she departed.

"In ten days we shall expect you at Pitlochry, " she said, smiling, to Arthur Meadows, as she swept past them in the corridor. Then, pausing, she held out a perfunctory hand to Doris.

"And we really can't persuade you to come too? "

The tone was careless and patronising. It brought the sudden red to Doris's cheek. For one moment she was tempted to say—"Thank you—since you are so kind—after all, why not? "—just that she might see the change in those large, malicious eyes—might catch their owner unawares, for once. But, as usual, nerve failed her. She merely said that her drawing would keep her all August in town; and that London, empty, was the best possible place for work. Lady Dunstable nodded and passed on.

The ten days flew. Meadows, kept to it by Doris, was very busy preparing another lecture for publication in an English review. Doris, meanwhile, got his clothes ready, and affected a uniformly cheerful and indifferent demeanour. On Arthur's last evening at home, however, he came suddenly into the sitting-room, where Doris was sewing on some final buttons, and after fidgeting about a little, with occasional glances at his wife, he said abruptly:

"I say, Doris, I won't go if you're going to take it like this. "

She turned upon him.

"Like what? "

"Oh, don't pretend! " was the impatient reply. "You know very well that you hate my going to Scotland! "

Doris, all on edge, and smarting under the too Jovian look and frown with which he surveyed her from the hearthrug, declared that, as it was not a case of her going to Scotland, but of his, she was entirely indifferent. If he enjoyed it, he was quite right to go. *She* was going to enjoy her work in Uncle Charles's studio.

Meadows broke out into an angry attack on her folly and unkindness. But the more he lost his temper, the more provokingly Doris kept hers. She sat there, surrounded by his socks and shirts, a trim, determined little figure—declining to admit that she was angry, or jealous, or offended, or anything of the kind. Would he please come upstairs and give her his last directions about his packing? She thought she had put everything ready; but there were just a few things she was doubtful about.

And all the time she seemed to be watching another Doris—a creature quite different from her real self. What had come over her? If anybody had told her beforehand that she could ever let slip her power over her own will like this, ever become possessed with this silent, obstinate demon of wounded love and pride, never would she have believed them! She moved under its grip like an automaton. She would not quarrel with Arthur. But as no soft confession was possible, and no mending or undoing of what had happened, to laugh her way through the difficult hours was all that remained. So that whenever Meadows renewed the attempt to "have it out, " he was met by renewed evasion and "chaff" on Doris's side, till he could only retreat with as much offended dignity as she allowed him.

It was after midnight before she had finished his packing. Then, bidding him a smiling good night, she fell asleep—apparently—as soon as her head touched the pillow.

The next morning, early, she stood on the steps waving farewell to Arthur, without a trace of ill-humour. And he, though vaguely uncomfortable, had submitted at last to what he felt was her fixed purpose of avoiding a scene. Moreover, the "eternal child" in him, which made both his charm and his weakness, had already scattered his compunctions of the preceding day, and was now aglow with the sheer joy of holiday and change. He had worked very hard, he had

had a great success, and now he was going to live for three weeks in the lap of luxury; intellectual luxury first and foremost—good talk, good company, an abundance of books for rainy days; but with the addition of a supreme *chef*, Lord Dunstable's champagne, and all the amenities of one of the best moors in Scotland.

Doris went back into the house, and, Arthur being no longer in the neighbourhood, allowed herself a few tears. She had never felt so lonely in her life, nor so humiliated. "My moral character is gone, " she said to herself. "I have no moral character. I thought I was a sensible, educated woman; and I am just an ''Arriet, ' in a temper with her ''Arry. ' Well—courage! Three weeks isn't long. Who can say that Arthur mayn't come back disillusioned? Rachel Dunstable is a born tyrant. If, instead of flattering him, she begins to bully him, strange things may happen! "

The first week of solitude she spent in household drudgery. Bills had to be paid, and there was now mercifully a little money to pay them with. Though it was August, the house was to be "spring-cleaned, " and Doris had made a compact with her sulky maids that when it began she would do no more than sleep and breakfast at home. She would spend her days in the Campden Hill studio, and sup on a tray—anywhere. On these terms, they grudgingly allowed her to occupy her own house.

The studio in which she worked was on the top of Campden Hill, and opened into one of the pleasant gardens of that neighbourhood. Her uncle, Charles Bentley, an elderly Academician, with an ugly, humorous face, red hair, red eyebrows, a black skull-cap, and a general weakness for the female sex, was very fond of his niece Doris, and inclined to think her a neglected and underrated wife. He was too fond of his own comfort, however, to let Meadows perceive this opinion of his; still less did he dare express it to Doris. All he could do was to befriend her and make her welcome at the studio, to advise her about her illustrations, and correct her drawing when it needed it. He himself was an old-fashioned artist, quite content to be "mid" or even "early" Victorian. He still cultivated the art of historical painting, and was still as anxious as any contemporary of Frith to tell a story. And as his manner was no less behind the age than his material, his pictures remained on his hands, while the "vicious horrors, " as they seemed to him, of the younger school held the field and captured the newspapers. But as he had some private means, and no kith or kin but his niece, the indifference of the public to his work caused him little disturbance. He pleased his own taste, allowing himself a good-natured contempt for the work which supplanted him, coupled with an ever-generous hand for any post-Impressionist in difficulties.

On the August afternoon when Doris, escaping at last from her maids and her accounts, made her way up to the studio, for some hours' work on the last three or four illustrations wanted for a Christmas book, Uncle Charles welcomed her with effusion.

"Where have you been, child, all this time? I thought you must have flitted entirely."

Doris explained—while she set up her easel—that for the first time in their lives she and Arthur had been seeing something of the great world, and—mildly—"doing" the season. Arthur was now continuing the season in Scotland, while she had stayed at home to work and rest. Throughout her talk, she avoided mentioning the Dunstables.

"H'm!" said Uncle Charles, "so you've been junketing!"

Doris admitted it.

"Did you like it?"

Doris put on her candid look.

"I daresay I should have liked it, if I'd made a success of it. Of course Arthur did."

"Too much trouble!" said the old painter, shaking his head. "I was in the swim, as they call it, for a year or two. I might have stayed there, I suppose, for I could always tell a story, and I wasn't afraid of the big-wigs. But I couldn't stand it. Dress-clothes are the deuce! And besides, talk now is not what it used to be. The clever men who can say smart things are too clever to say them. Nobody wants 'em! So let's 'cultivate our garden, ' my dear, and be thankful. I'm beginning a new picture—and I've found a topping new model. What can a man want more? Very nice of you to let Arthur go, and have his head. Where is it? —some smart moor? He'll soon be tired of it."

Doris laughed, let the question as to the "smart moor" pass, and came round to look at the new subject that Uncle Charles was laying in. He explained it to her, well knowing that he spoke to unsympathetic ears, for whatever Doris might draw for her publishers, she was a passionate and humble follower of those modern experimentalists who have made the Slade School famous. The subject was, it seemed, to be a visit paid to Joanna the mad and widowed mother of Charles V., at Tordesillas, by the envoys of Henry VII., who were thus allowed by Ferdinand, the Queen's father, to convince themselves that the Queen's profound melancholia formed an insuperable barrier to the marriage proposals of the English King. The figure of the distracted Queen, crouching in white beside a window from which she could see the tomb of her dead and adored husband, the Archduke Philip, and some of the splendid figures of the English embassy, were already sketched.

"I have been fit to hang myself over her! " said Bentley, pointing to the Queen. "I tried model after model. At last I've got the very thing! She comes to-day for the first time. You'll see her! Before she comes, I must scrape out Joanna, so as to look at the thing quite fresh. But I daresay I shall only make a few sketches of the lady to-day."

"Who is she, and where did you get her! "

Bentley laughed. "You won't like her, my dear! Never mind. Her appearance is magnificent—whatever her mind and morals may be. "

And he described how he had heard of the lady from an artist friend who had originally seen her at a music-hall, and had persuaded her to come and sit to him. The comic haste and relief with which he had now transferred her to Bentley lost nothing in Bentley's telling. Of course she had "a fiend of a temper. " "Wish you joy of her! Oh, don't ask me about her! You'll find out for yourself. " "I can manage her, " said Uncle Charles tranquilly. "I've had so many of 'em. "

"She is Spanish? "

"Not at all. She is Italian. That is to say, her mother was a Neapolitan, the daughter of a jeweller in Hatton Garden, and her father an English bank clerk. The Neapolitans have a lot of Spanish blood in them—hence, no doubt, the physique. "

"And she is a professional model!"

"Nothing of the sort! —though she will probably become one. She is a writer—Heaven save the mark! —and I have to pay her vast sums to get her. It is the greatest favour."

"A *writer*?"

"Poetess! —and journalist!" said Uncle Charles, enjoying Doris's puzzled look. "She sent me her poems yesterday. As to journalism"—his eyes twinkled—"I say nothing—but this. Watch her *hats*! She has the reputation—in certain circles—of being the best-hatted woman in London. All this I get from the man who handed her on to me. As I said to him, it depends on what 'London' you mean."

"Married?"

"Oh dear no, though of course she calls herself 'Madame' like the rest of them—Madame Vavasour. I have reason, however, to believe that her real name is Flink—Elena Flink. And I should say—very much on the look-out for a husband; and meanwhile very much courted by boys—who go to what she calls her 'evenings.' It is odd, the taste that some youths have for these elderly Circes."

"Elderly?" said Doris, busy the while with her own preparations. "I was hoping for something young and beautiful!"

"Young? —no! —an unmistakable thirty-five. Beautiful? Well, wait till you see her... H'm—that shoulder won't do!"—Doris had just placed a preliminary sketch of one of her "subjects" under his eyes—"and that bit of perspective in the corner wants a lot of seeing to. Look here!" The old Academician, brought up in the spirit of Ingres—"le dessin, c'est la probité! —le dessin, c'est l'honneur!"—fell eagerly to work on the sketch, and Doris watched.

They were both absorbed, when there was a knock at the door. Doris turned hastily, expecting to see the model. Instead of which there entered, in response to Bentley's "Come in!" a girl of four or five and twenty, in a blue linen dress and a shady hat, who nodded a quiet "Good afternoon" to the artist, and proceeded at once with an air of business to a writing-table at the further end of the studio, covered with papers.

"Miss Wigram, " said the artist, raising his voice, "let me introduce you to my niece, Mrs. Meadows. "

The girl rose from her chair again and bowed. Then Doris saw that she had a charming tired face, beautiful eyes on which she had just placed spectacles, and soft brown hair framing her thin cheeks.

"A novelty since you were here, " whispered Bentley in Doris's ear. "She's an accountant—capital girl! Since these Liberal budgets came along, I can't keep my own accounts, or send in my own income-tax returns—dash them! So she does the whole business for me—pays everything—sees to everything—comes once a week. We shall all be run by the women soon! "

* * * * *

The studio had grown very quiet. Through some glass doors open to the garden came in little wandering winds which played with some loose papers on the floor, and blew Doris's hair about her eyes as she stooped over her easel, absorbed in her drawing. Apparently absorbed: her subliminal mind, at least, was far away, wandering on a craggy Scotch moor. A lady on a Scotch pony—she understood that Lady Dunstable often rode with the shooters—and a tall man walking beside her, carrying, not a gun, but a walking stick: —that was the vision in the crystal. Arthur was too bad a shot to be tolerated in the Dunstable circle; had indeed wisely announced from the beginning that he was not to be included among the guns. All the more time for conversation, the give and take of wits, the pleasures of the intellectual tilting-ground; the whole watered by good wine, seasoned with the best of cooking, and lapped in the general ease of a house where nobody ever thought of such a vulgar thing as money except to spend it.

Doris had in general a severe mind as to the rich and aristocratic classes. Her own hard and thrifty life had disposed her to see them *en noir*. But the sudden rush of a certain section of them to crowd Arthur's lectures had been certainly mollifying. If it had not been for the Vampire, Doris was well aware that her standards might have given way.

As it was, Lady Dunstable's exacting ways, her swoop, straight and fierce, on the social morsel she desired, like that of an eagle on the sheepfold, had made her, in Doris's sore consciousness, the representative of thousands more; all greedy, able, domineering, inevitably getting what they wanted, and more than they deserved; against whom the starved and virtuous intellectuals of the professional classes were bound to contend to the death. The story of that poor girl, that clergyman's daughter, for instance—could anything have been more insolent—more cruel? Doris burned to avenge her.

Suddenly—a great clatter and noise in the passage leading from the small house behind to the studio and garden.

"Here she is! "

Uncle Charles sprang up, and reached the studio door just as a shower of knocks descended upon it from outside. He opened it, and on the threshold there stood two persons; a stout lady in white, surmounted by a huge black hat with a hearse-like array of plumes; and, behind her, a tall and willowy youth, with—so far as could be seen through the chinks of the hat—a large nose, fair hair, pale blue eyes, and a singular deficiency of chin. He carried in his arms a tiny black Spitz with a pink ribbon round its neck.

The lady looked, frowning, into the interior of the studio. She held in her hand a very large fan, with the handle of which she had been rapping the door; and the black feathers with which she was canopied seemed to be nodding in her eyes.

"Maestro, you are not alone! " she said in a deep, reproachful voice.

"My niece, Mrs. Meadows—Madame Vavasour, " said Bentley, ushering in the new-comer.

Doris turned from her easel and bowed, only to receive a rather scowling response.

"And your friend? " As he spoke the artist looked blandly at the young man.

"I brought him to amuse me, Maestro. When I am dull my countenance changes, and you cannot do it justice. He will talk to me—I shall be animated—and you will profit. "

"Ah, no doubt! " said Bentley, smiling. "And your friend's name? "

"Herbert Dunstable—Honourable Herbert Dunstable! —Signor Bentley," said Madame Vavasour, advancing with a stately step into the room, and waving peremptorily to the young man to follow.

Doris sat transfixed and staring. Bentley turned to look at his niece, and their eyes met—his full of suppressed mirth. The son! —the unsatisfactory son! Doris remembered that his name was Herbert. In the train of this third-rate sorceress!

Her thoughts ran excitedly to the distant moors, and that magnificent lady, with her circle of distinguished persons, holiday-making statesmen, peers, diplomats, writers, and the like. Here was a humbler scene! But Doris's fancy at once divined a score of links between it and the high comedy yonder.

Meanwhile, at the name of Dunstable, the girl accountant in the distance had also moved sharply, so as to look at the young man. But in the bustle of Madame Vavasour's entrance, and her passage to the sitter's chair, the girl's gesture passed unnoticed.

"I'm just worn out, Maestro!" said the model languidly, uplifting a pair of tragic eyes to the artist. "I sat up half the night writing. I had a subject which tormented me. But I have done something *splendid*! Isn't it splendid, Herbert?"

"Ripping!" said the young man, grinning widely.

"Sit down!" said Madame, with a change of tone. And the youth sat down, on the very low chair to which she pointed him, doing his best to dispose of his long legs.

"Give me the dog!" she commanded. "You have no idea how to hold him—poor lamb!"

The dog was handed to her; she took off her enormous hat with many sighs of fatigue, and then, with the dog on her lap, asked how she was to sit. Bentley explained that he wished to make a few preliminary sketches of her head and bust, and proceeded to pose her. She accepted his directions with a curious pettishness, as though they annoyed her; and presently complained loudly that the chair was uncomfortable, and the pose irksome. He handled her, however, with a good-humoured mixture of flattery and persuasion, and at last, stepping back, surveyed the result—well content.

There was no doubt whatever that she was a very handsome woman, and that her physical type—that of the more lethargic and heavily built Neapolitan—suggested very happily the mad and melancholy Queen. She had superb black hair, eyes profoundly dark, a low and beautiful brow, lips classically fine, a powerful head and neck, and a complexion which, but for the treatment given it, would have been of a clear and beautiful olive. She wore a draggled dress of cream-coloured muslin, very transparent over the shoulders, somewhat scandalously wanting at the throat and breast, and very frayed and dirty round the skirt. Her feet, which were large and plump, were cased in extremely pointed shoes with large paste buckles; and as she crossed them on the stool provided for them she showed a considerable amount of rather clumsy ankle. The hands too were large, common, and ill-kept, and the wrists laden with bracelets. She was adorned indeed with a great deal of jewellery, including some startling earrings of a bright green stone. The hat, which she had carefully placed on a chair beside her, was truly a monstrosity!—but, as Doris guessed, an expensive monstrosity, such as the Rue de la Paix provides, at anything from a hundred and fifty to two hundred and fifty francs, for those of its cosmopolitan customers whom it pillages and despises. How did the lady afford it? The rest of her dress suggested a struggle with small means, waged by one who was greedy for effect, obtained at a minimum of trouble. That she was rouged and powdered goes without saying.

And the young man? Doris perceived at once his likeness to his father—a feeble likeness. But he was evidently simple and good-natured, and to all appearance completely in the power of the enchantress. He fanned her assiduously. He picked up all the various belongings—gloves, handkerchiefs, handbag—which she perpetually let fall. He ran after the dog whenever it escaped from the lady's lap and threatened mischief in the studio; and by way of amusing her—the purpose for which he had been imported—he kept up a stream of small cryptic gossip about various common acquaintances, most of whom seemed to belong to the music-hall profession, and to be either "stars" or the satellites of "stars." Madame listened to him with avidity, and occasionally broke into a giggling laugh. She had, however, two manners, and two kinds of conversation, which she adopted with the young man and the Academician respectively. Her talk with the youth suggested the jealous ascendency of a coarse-minded woman. She occasionally flattered him, but more generally she teased or "ragged" him. She seemed indeed to feel him securely in her grip; so that there was no need to pose for him, as—figuratively as well as physically—she posed for Bentley. To the artist she gave her opinions on pictures or books—on the novels of Mr. Wells, or the plays of Mr. Bernard Shaw—in the languid or drawling tone of accepted authority; dropping every now and then into a broad cockney accent, which produced a startling effect, like that of unexpected garlic in cookery. Bentley's gravity was often severely tried, and Doris altered the position of her own easel so that he and she could not see each other. Meanwhile Madame took not the smallest notice of Mr. Bentley's niece, and Doris made no advances to the young man, to whom her name was clearly quite unknown. Had Circe really got him in her toils? Doris judged him soft-headed and soft-hearted; no match at all for the lady. The thought of her walking the lawns or the drawing-rooms of Crosby Ledgers as the betrothed of the heir stirred in Arthur Meadows's wife a silent, and—be it confessed! —a malicious convulsion. Such mothers, so self-centred, so set on their own triumphs, with their intellectual noses so very much in the clouds, deserved such sons! She promised herself to keep her own counsel, and watch the play.

The sitting lasted for two hours. When it was over, Uncle Charles, all smiles and satisfaction, went with his visitors to the front door.

He was away some little time, and returned, bubbling, to the studio.

"She's been cross-examining me about her poems! I had to confess I hadn't read a word of them. And now she's offered to recite next time she comes! Good Heavens—how can I get out of it? I believe, Doris, she's hooked that young idiot! She told me she was engaged to him. Do you know anything of his people?"

The girl accountant suddenly came forward. She looked flushed and distressed.

"I do!" she said, with energy. "Can't somebody stop that? It will break their hearts!"

Doris and Uncle Charles looked at her in amazement.

"Whose hearts?" said the painter.

"Lord and Lady Dunstable's."

"You know them?" exclaimed Doris.

"I used to know them—quite well," said the girl, quietly. "My father had one of Lord Dunstable's livings. He died last year. He didn't like Lady Dunstable. He quarrelled with her, because—because she once did a very rude thing to me. But this would be *too* awful! And poor Lord Dunstable! Everybody likes him. Oh—it must be stopped! —it *must*!"

CHAPTER IV

When Doris reached home that evening, the little Kensington house, with half its carpets up and all but two of its rooms under dust-sheets, looked particularly lonely and unattractive. Arthur's study was unrecognisable. No cheerful litter anywhere. No smell of tobacco, no sign of a male presence! Doris, walking restlessly from room to room, had never felt so forsaken, so dismally certain that the best of life was done. Moreover, she had fully expected to find a letter from Arthur waiting for her; and there was nothing.

It was positively comic that under such circumstances anybody should expect her—Doris Meadows—to trouble her head about Lady Dunstable's affairs. Of course she would feel it if her son made a ridiculous and degrading marriage. But why not? —why shouldn't he come to grief like anybody else's son? Why should heaven and earth be moved in order to prevent it? —especially by the woman to whose possible jealousy and pain Lady Dunstable had certainly never given the most passing thought.

All the same, the distress shown by that odd girl, Miss Wigram, and her appeal both to the painter and his niece to intervene and save the foolish youth, kept echoing in Doris's memory, although neither she nor Bentley had received it with any cordiality. Doris had soon made out that this girl, Alice Wigram, was indeed the clergyman's daughter whom Lady Dunstable had snubbed so unkindly some twelve months before. She was evidently a sweet-natured, susceptible creature, to whom Lord Dunstable had taken a fancy, in his fatherly way, during occasional visits to her father's rectory, and of whom he had spoken to his wife. That Lady Dunstable should have unkindly slighted this motherless girl, who had evidently plenty of natural capacity under her shyness, was just like her, and Doris's feelings of antagonism to the tyrant were only sharpened by her acquaintance with the victim. Why should Miss Wigram worry her self? Lord Dunstable? Well, but after all, capable men should keep such wives in order. If Lord Dunstable had not been scandalously weak, Lady Dunstable would not have become a terror to her sex.

As for Uncle Charles, he had simply declined all responsibility in the matter. He had never seen the Dunstables, wouldn't know them from Adam, and had no concern whatever in what happened to their son. The situation merely excited in him one man's natural amusement at the folly of another. The boy was more than of age. Really he and his mother must look after themselves. To meddle with the young man's love affairs, simply because he happened to visit your studio in the company of a lady, would be outrageous. So the painter laughed, shook his head, and went back to his picture. Then Miss Wigram, looking despondently from the silent Doris to the artist at work, had said with sudden energy, "I must find out about her! I'm—I'm sure she's a horrid woman! Can you tell me, sir"—she addressed Bentley—"the name of the gentleman who was painting her before she came here?"

Bentley had hummed and hawed a little, twisting his red moustache, and finally had given the name and address; whereupon Miss Wigram had gathered up her papers, some of which had drifted to the floor between her table and Doris's easel, and had taken an immediate departure, a couple of hours before her usual time, throwing, as she left the studio, a wistful and rather puzzled look at Mrs. Meadows.

Doris congratulated herself that she had kept her own counsel on the subject of the Dunstables, both with Uncle Charles and Miss Wigram. Neither of them had guessed that she had any personal acquaintance with them. She tried now to put the matter out of her thoughts. Jane brought in a tray for her mistress, and Doris supped meagrely in Arthur's deserted study, thinking, as the sunset light came in across the dusty street, of that flame and splendour which such weather must be kindling on the moors, of the blue and purple distances, the glens of rocky mountains hung in air, "the gleam, the shadow, and the peace supreme"! She remembered how on their September honeymoon they had wandered in Ross-shire, how the whole land was dyed crimson by the heather, and how impossible it was to persuade Arthur to walk discreetly rather than, like any cockney tripper, with his arm round his sweetheart. Scotland had not been far behind the Garden of Eden under those circumstances. But Arthur was now pursuing the higher, the intellectual joys.

She finished her supper, and then sat down to write to her husband. Was she going to tell him anything about the incident of the afternoon? Why should she? Why should she give him the chance of becoming more than ever Lady Dunstable's friend—pegging out an eternal claim upon her gratitude?

Doris wrote her letter. She described the progress of the spring cleaning; she reported that her sixth illustration was well forward, and that Uncle Charles was wrestling with another historical picture, a *machine* neither better nor worse than all the others. She thought that after all Jane would soon give warning; and she, Doris, had spent three pounds in petty cash since he went away; how, she could not remember, but it was all in her account book.

And she concluded:

I understand then that we meet at Crewe on Friday fortnight? I have heard of a lodging near Capel Curig which sounds delightful. We might do a week's climbing and then go on to the sea. I really *shall* want a holiday. Has there not been ten minutes even—since you arrived—to write a letter in? —or a postcard? Shall I send you a few addressed?

Having thus finished what seemed to her the dullest letter she had ever written in her life, she looked at it a while, irresolutely, then put it in an envelope hastily, addressed, stamped it, and rang the bell for Jane to run across the street with it and post it. After which, she sat idle a little while with flushed cheeks, while the twilight gathered.

* * * * *

The gate of the trim front garden swung on its hinges. Doris turned to look. She saw, to her astonishment, that the girl-accountant of the morning, Miss Wigram, was coming up the flagged path to the house. What could she want?

"Oh, Mrs. Meadows—I'm so sorry to disturb you—" said the visitor, in some agitation, as Doris, summoned by Jane, entered the dust-sheeted drawing-room. "But you dropped an envelope with an address this afternoon. I picked it up with some of my papers and never discovered it till I got home. "

She held out the envelope. Doris took it, and flushed vividly. It was the envelope with his Scotch address which Arthur had written out for her before leaving home—"care of the Lord Dunstable, Franick Castle, Pitlochry, Perthshire, N.B. " She had put it in her portfolio, out of which it had no doubt slipped while she was at work.

She and Miss Wigram eyed each other. The girl was evidently agitated. But she seemed not to know how to begin what she had to say.

Doris broke the silence.

"You were astonished to find that I know the Dunstables?"

"Oh, no! —I didn't think—" stammered her visitor—"I supposed some friend of yours might be staying there."

"My husband is staying there," said Doris, quietly. Really it was too much trouble to tell a falsehood. Her pride refused.

"Oh, I see!" cried Miss Wigram, though in fact she was more bewildered than before. Why should this extraordinary little lady have behaved at the studio as if she had never heard of the Dunstables, and be now confessing that her husband was actually staying in their house?

Doris smiled—with perfect self-possession.

"Please sit down. You think it odd, of course, that I didn't tell you I knew the Dunstables, while we were talking about them. The fact is I didn't want to be mixed up with the affair at all. We have only lately made acquaintance with the Dunstables. Lady Dunstable is my husband's friend. I don't like her very much. But neither of us knows her well enough to go and tell her tales about her son."

Miss Wigram considered—her gentle, troubled eyes bent upon Doris. "Of course—I know—how many people dislike Lady Dunstable. She did a—rather cruel thing to me once. The thought of it humiliated and discouraged me for a long time. It made me almost glad to leave home. And of course she hasn't won Mr. Herbert's confidence at all. She has always snubbed and disapproved of him. Oh, I knew him very little. I have hardly ever spoken to him. You saw he didn't recognise me this afternoon. But my father used to go over to Crosby Ledgers to coach him in the holidays, and he often told me that as a boy he was *terrified* of his mother. She either took no notice of him at all, or she was always sneering at him, and scolding him. As soon as ever he came of age and got a little money of his own, he declared he wouldn't live at home. His father wanted him to go into Parliament or the army, but he said he hated the army, and if he was such a dolt as his mother thought him it would be ridiculous to attempt politics. And so he just drifted up to town and looked out for people that would make much of him, and wouldn't snub him. And that, of course, was how he got into the toils of a woman like that!"

The girl threw up her hands tragically.

Doris sat up, with energy.

"But what on earth, " she said, "does it matter to you or to me?"

"Oh, can't you see?" said the other, flushing deeply, and with the tears in her eyes. "My father had one of Lord Dunstable's livings. We lived on that estate for years. Everybody loved Lord Dunstable. And though Lady Dunstable makes enemies, there's a great respect for the *family*. They've been there since Queen Elizabeth's time. And it's *dreadful* to think of a woman like—well, like that!—reigning at Crosby Ledgers. I think of the poor people. Lady Dunstable's good to them; though of course you wouldn't hear anything about it, unless you lived there. She tries to do her duty to them—she really does—in her own way. And, of course, they *respect* her. No Dunstable has ever done anything disgraceful! Isn't there something in *'Noblesse oblige'? Think* of this woman at the head of that estate!"

"Well, upon my word, " said Doris, after a pause, "you *are* feudal. Don't you feel yourself that you are old-fashioned?"

Mrs. Meadows's half-sarcastic look at first intimidated her visitor, and then spurred her into further attempts to explain herself.

"I daresay it's old-fashioned, " she said slowly, "but I'm sure it's what father would have felt. Anyway, I went off to try and find out what I could. I went first to a little club I belong to—for professional women—near the Strand, and I asked one or two women I found there—who know artists—and models—and write for papers. And very soon I found out a great deal. I didn't have to go to the man whose address Mr. Bentley gave me. Madame Vavasour *is* a horrid woman! This is not the first young man she's fleeced—by a long way. There was a man—younger than Mr. Dunstable, a boy of nineteen—three years ago. She got him to promise to marry her; and the parents came down, and paid her enormously to let him go. Now she's got through all that money, and she boasts she's going to marry young Dunstable before his parents know anything about it. She's going to make sure of a peerage this time. Oh, she's odious! She's greedy, she's vulgar, she's false! And of course"—the girl's eyes grew wide and scared—"there may be other things much worse. How do we know?"

"How do we know indeed!" said Doris, with a shrug. "Well!"—she turned her eyes full upon her guest—"and what are you going to do?"

An eager look met hers.

"Couldn't you—couldn't you write to Mr. Meadows, and ask him to warn Lady Dunstable?"

Doris shook her head.

"Why don't you do it yourself?"

The girl flushed uncomfortably. "You see, father quarrelled with her about that unkind thing she did to me—oh, it isn't worth telling! — but he wrote her an angry letter, and they never spoke afterwards. Lady Dunstable never forgives that kind of thing. If people find fault with her, she just drops them. I don't believe she'd read a letter from me!"

"*Les offensés*, etc.," said Doris, meditating. "But what are the facts? Has the boy actually promised to marry her? She may have been telling lies to my uncle."

"She tells everybody so. I saw a girl who knows her quite well. They write for the same paper—it's a fashion paper. You saw that hat, by the way, she had on? She gets them as perquisites from the smart shops she writes about. She has a whole cupboard of them at home, and when she wants money she sells them for what she can get. Well, she told me that Madame—they all call her Madame, though they all know quite well that she's not married, and that her name is Flink—boasts perpetually of her engagement. It seems that he was ill in the winter—in his lodgings. His mother knew nothing about it— he wouldn't tell her, and Madame nursed him, and made a fuss of him. And Mr. Dunstable thought he owed her a great deal—and she made scenes and told him she had compromised herself by coming to nurse him—and all that kind of nonsense. And at last he promised to marry her—in writing. And now she's so sure of him that she just bullies him—you saw how she ordered him about to-day."

"Well, why doesn't he marry her, if he's such a fool—why hasn't he married her long ago?" cried Doris.

Miss Wigram looked distressed.

"I don't know. My friend thinks it's his father. She believes, at least, that he doesn't want to get married without telling Lord Dunstable; and that, of course, means telling his mother. And he hates the thought of the letters and the scenes. So he keeps it hanging on; and lately Madame has been furious with him, and is always teasing and sniffing at him. He's dreadfully weak, and my friend's afraid that before he's made up his own mind what to do that woman will have carried him off to a registry office—and got the horrid thing done for good and all."

There was silence a moment. After which Doris said, with a cold decision:

"You can't imagine how absurd it seems to me that you should come and ask me to help Lady Dunstable with her son. There is nobody in the world less helpless than Lady Dunstable, and nobody who would be less grateful for being helped. I really cannot meddle with it."

She rose as she spoke, and Miss Wigram rose too.

"Couldn't you—couldn't you—" said the girl pleadingly—"just ask Mr. Meadows to warn Lord Dunstable? I'm thinking of the villagers, and the farmers, and the schools—all the people we used to love. Father was there twenty years! To think of the dear place given over—some day—to that creature!"

Her charming eyes actually filled with tears. Doris was touched, but at the same time set on edge. This loyalty that people born and bred in the country feel to our English country system—what an absurd and unreal frame of mind! And when our country system produces Lady Dunstables!

"They have such a pull!"—she thought angrily—"such a hideously unfair pull, over other people! The way everybody rushes to help them when they get into a mess—to pick up the pieces—and sweep it all up! It's irrational—it's sickening! Let them look after themselves—and pay for their own misdeeds like the rest of us."

"I can't interfere—I really can't!" she said, straightening her slim shoulders. "It is not as though we were old friends of Lord and Lady Dunstable. Don't you see how very awkward it would be? Let me advise you just to watch the thing a little, and then to apply to somebody in the Crosby Ledgers neighbourhood. You must have some friends or acquaintances there, who at any rate could do more than we could. And perhaps after all it's a mare's nest, and the young man doesn't mean to marry her at all!"

The girl's anxious eyes scanned Doris's unyielding countenance; then with a sigh she gave up her attempt, and said "Good-bye." Doris went with her to the door.

"We shall meet to-morrow, shan't we?" she said, feeling a vague compunction. "And I suppose this woman will be there again. You can keep an eye on her. Are you living alone—or are you with friends?"

"Oh, I'm in a boarding-house," said Miss Wigram, hastily. Then as though she recognised the new softness in Doris's look, she added, "I'm quite comfortable there—and I've a great deal of work. Good night."

* * * * *

"All alone!—with that gentle face—and that terrible amount of conscience—hard lines!" thought Doris, as she reflected on her visitor. "I felt a black imp beside her!"

All the same, the letter which Mrs. Meadows received by the following morning's post was not at all calculated to melt the "black imp" further. Arthur wrote in a great hurry to beg that she would not go on with their Welsh plans—for the moment.

Lady D— — has insisted on my going on a short yachting cruise with her and Miss Field, the week after next. She wants to show me the West Coast, and they have a small cottage in the Shetlands where we should stay a night or two and watch the sea-birds. It *may* keep me away another week or fortnight, but you won't mind, dear, will you?

I am getting famously rested, and really the house is very agreeable. In these surroundings Lady Dunstable is less of the *bas-bleu*, and more of the woman. You *must* make up your mind to come another year! You would soon get over your prejudice and make friends with her. She looks after us all—she talks brilliantly—and I haven't seen her rude to anybody since I arrived. There are some very nice people here, and altogether I am enjoying it. Don't you work too hard—and don't let the servants harry you. Post just going. Good night!

Another week or fortnight! —five weeks, or nearly, altogether. Doris was sorely wounded. She went to look at herself in the mirror over the chimney-piece. Was she not thin and haggard for want of rest and holiday? Would not the summer weather be all done by the time Arthur graciously condescended to come back to her? Were there not dark lines under her eyes, and was she not feeling a limp and wretched creature, unfit for any exertion? What was wrong with her? She hated her drawing—she hated everything. And there was Arthur, proposing to go yachting with Lady Dunstable! —while she might toil and moil—all alone—in this August London! The tears rushed into her eyes. Her pride only just saved her from a childish fit of crying.

But in the end resentment came to her aid, together with an angry and redoubled curiosity as to what might be happening to Lady Dunstable's precious son while Lady Dunstable was thus absorbed in robbing other women of their husbands. Doris hurried her small household affairs, that she might get off early to the studio; and as she put on her hat, her fancy drew vindictive pictures of the scene which any day might realise—the scene at Franick Castle, when Lady Dunstable, unsuspecting, should open the letter which announced to her the advent of her daughter-in-law, Elena, *née* Flink—or should gather the same unlovely fact from a casual newspaper paragraph. As for interfering between her and her rich deserts, Doris vowed to herself she would not lift a finger. That incredibly forgiving young woman, Miss Wigram, might do as she pleased. But when a mother pursues her own selfish ends so as to make her only son dislike and shun her, let her take what comes. It was in the mood of an Erinnys that Doris made her way northwards to Campden Hill, and nobody perceiving the slight erect figure in the corner of the omnibus could possibly have guessed at the storm within.

A Great Success

The August day was hot and lifeless. Heat mist lay over the park, and over the gardens on the slopes of Campden Hill. Doris could hardly drag her weary feet along, as she walked from where the omnibus had set her down to her uncle's studio. But it was soon evident that within the studio itself there was animation enough. From the long passage approaching it Doris heard someone shouting—declaiming—what appeared to be verse. Madame, of course, reciting her own poems—poor Uncle Charles! Doris stopped outside the door, which was slightly open, to listen, and heard these astonishing lines—delivered very slowly and pompously, in a thick, strained voice:

> "My heart is adamant! The tear-drops drip and drip—
> Force their slow path, and tear their desperate way.
> The vulture Pain sits close, to snip—and snip—and snip
> My sad, sweet life to ruin—well-a-day!
> I am deceived—a bleating lamb bereft!—who goes
> Baa-baaing to the moon o'er lonely lands.
> Through all my shivering veins a tender fervour flows;
> I cry to Love—'Reach out, my Lord, thy hands!
> And save me from these ugly beasts who ramp and rage
> Around me all day long—beasts fell and sore—
> Envy, and Hate, and Calumny!—do thou assuage
> Their impious mouths, O splendid Love, and floor
> Their hideous tactics, and their noisome spleen,
> Withering to dust the awful "Might-Have-Been!"'"

"Goodness! 'Howls the Sublime' indeed! " thought Doris, gurgling with laughter in the passage. As soon as she had steadied her face she opened the studio door, and perceived Lady Dunstable's prospective daughter-in-law standing in the middle of the studio, head thrown back and hands outstretched, invoking the Cyprian. The shriek of the first lines had died away in a stage whisper; the reciter was glaring fiercely into vacancy.

Doris's merry eyes devoured the scene. On the chair from which the model had risen she had deposited yet another hat, so large, so audacious and beplumed that it seemed to have a positive personality, a positive swagger of its own, and to be winking roguishly at the audience. Meanwhile Madame's muslin dress of the day before had been exchanged for something more appropriate to the warmth of her poetry—a tawdry flame-coloured satin, in which her "too, too solid" frame was tightly sheathed. Her coal-black hair, tragically wild, looked as though no comb had been near it for a month, and the gloves drawn half-way up the bare arms hardly remembered they had ever been white.

A slovenly, dishevelled, vulgar woman, reciting bombastic nonsense! And yet! —a touch of Southern magnificence, even of Southern grace, amid the cockney squalor and finery. Doris coolly recognised it, as she stood, herself invisible, behind her uncle's large easel. Thence she perceived also the other persons in the studio: — Bentley sitting in front of the poetess, hiding his eyes with one hand, and nervously tapping the arm of his chair with the other; to the right of him—seen sideways—the lanky form, flushed face, and open mouth of young Dunstable; and in the far distance, Miss Wigram.

Then—a surprising thing! The awkward pause following the recitation was suddenly broken by a loud and uncontrollable laugh. Doris, startled, turned to look at young Dunstable. For it was he who had laughed. Madame also shook off her stage trance to look—a thunderous frown upon her handsome face. The young man laughed on—laughed hysterically—burying his face in his hands. Madame Vavasour—all attitudes thrown aside—ran up to him in a fury.

"Why are you laughing? You insult me! —you have done it before. And now before strangers—it is too much! I insist that you explain!"

She stood over him, her eyes blazing. The youth, still convulsed, did his best to quiet the paroxysm which had seized him, and at last said, gasping:

"I was—I was thinking—of your reciting that at Crosby Ledgers—to my mother—and—and what she would say."

Even under her rouge it could be seen that the poetess turned a grey white.

"And pray—what would she say?"

The question was delivered with apparent calm. But Madame's eyes were dangerous. Doris stepped forward. Her uncle stayed her with a gesture. He himself rose, but Madame fiercely waved him aside. Miss Wigram, in the distance, had also moved forward—and paused.

"What would she say?" demanded Madame, again—at the sword's point.

"I—I don't know—" said young Dunstable, helplessly, still shaking. "I—I think—she'd laugh."

And he went off again, hysterically, trying in vain to stop the fit. Madame bit her lip. Then came a torrent of Italian—evidently a torrent of abuse; and then she lifted a gloved hand and struck the young man violently on the cheek.

"Take that! —you insolent—you—you barbarian! You are my *fiancé*, —my promised husband—and you mock at me; you will encourage your stuck-up mother to mock at me—I know you will! But I tell you—"

The speaker, however, had stopped abruptly, and instead of saying anything more she fell back panting, her eyes on the young man. For Herbert Dunstable had risen. At the blow, an amazing change had passed over his weak countenance and weedy frame. He put his hand to his forehead a moment, as though trying to collect his thoughts, and then he turned—quietly—to look for his hat and stick.

"Where are you going, Herbert?" stammered Madame. "I—I was carried away—I forgot myself!"

"I think not," said the young man, who was extremely pale. "This is not the first time. I bid you good morning, Madame—and good-bye!"

He stood looking at the now frightened woman, with a strange, surprised look, like one just emerging from a semi-conscious state; and in that moment, as Doris seemed to perceive, the traditions of his birth and breeding had returned upon him; something instinctive and inherited had reappeared; and the gentlemanly, easy-going father, who yet, as Doris remembered, when matters were serious "always got his way," was there—strangely there—in the degenerate son.

"Where are you going?" repeated Madame, eyeing him. "You promised to give me lunch."

"I regret—I have an engagement. Mr. Bentley—when the sitting is over—will you kindly see—Miss Flink—into a taxi? I thank you very much for allowing me to come and watch your work. I trust the picture will be a success. Good-bye! "

He held out his hand to Bentley, and bowed to Doris. Madame made a rush at him. But Bentley held her back. He seized her arms, indeed, quietly but irresistibly, while the young man made his retreat. Then, with a shriek, Madame fell back on her chair, pretending to faint, and Bentley, in no hurry, went to her assistance, while Doris slipped out after young Dunstable. She overtook him on the door-step.

"Mr. Dunstable, may I speak to you? "

He turned in astonishment, showing a grim pallor which touched her pity.

"I know your mother and father, " said Doris hurriedly; "at least my husband and I were staying at Crosby Ledges some weeks ago, and my husband is now in Scotland with your people. His name is Arthur Meadows. I am Mrs. Meadows. I—I don't know whether I could help you. You seem"—her smile flashed out—"to be in a horrid mess! "

The young man looked in perplexity at the small, trim lady before him, as though realising her existence for the first time. Her honest eyes were bent upon him with the same expression she had often worn when Arthur had come to her with some confession of folly— the expression which belongs to the maternal side of women, and is at once mocking and sweet. It said—"Of course you are a great fool! —most men are. But that's the *raison d'être* of women! Suppose we go into the business! "

"You're very kind—" he groaned—"awfully kind. I'm ashamed you should have seen—such a thing. Nobody can help me—thank you very much. I am engaged to that lady—I've promised to marry her. Oh, she's got any amount of evidence. I've been an ass—and worse. But I can't get out of it. I don't mean to try to get out of it. I promised of my own free will. Only I've found out now I can never live with her. Her temper is fiendish. It degrades her—and me. But you saw! She has made my life a burden to me lately, because I wouldn't name a day for us to be married. I wanted to see my father quietly first—without my mother knowing—and I have been thinking how to manage it—and funking it of course—I always do funk things. But what she did just now has settled it—it has been blowing up for a long time. I shall marry her—at a registry office—as soon as possible. Then I shall separate from her, and—I hope—never see her again. The lawyers will arrange that—and money! Thank you—it's awfully good of you to want to help me—but you can't—nobody can."

Doris had drawn her companion into her uncle's small dining-room and closed the door. She listened to his burst of confidence with a puzzled concern.

"Why must you marry her?" she said abruptly, when he paused. "Break it off! It would be far best."

"No. I promised. I—" he stammered a little—"I seem to have done her harm—her reputation, I mean. There is only one thing could let me off. She swore to me that—well!—that she was a good woman—that there was nothing in her past—you understand—"

"And you know of nothing?" said Doris, gravely.

"Nothing. And you don't think I'm going to try and ferret out things against her!" cried the youth, flushing. "No—I must just bear it."

"It's your parents that will have to bear it!"

His face hardened.

"My mother might have prevented it," he said bitterly. "However, I won't go into that. My father will see I couldn't do anything else. I'd better get it over. I'm going to my lawyers now. They'll take a few days over what I want."

"You'll tell your father?"

"I—I don't know," he said, irresolutely. She noticed that he did not try to pledge her not to give him away. And she, on her side, did not threaten to do so. She argued with him a little more, trying to get at his real thoughts, and to straighten them out for him. But it was evident he had made up such mind as he had, and that his sudden resolution—even the ugly scene which had made him take it—had been a relief. He knew at last where he stood.

A Great Success

So presently Doris let him go. They parted, liking each other decidedly. He thanked her warmly—though drearily—for taking an interest in him, and he said to her on the threshold:

"Some day, I hope, you'll come to Crosby Ledgers again, Mrs. Meadows—and I'll be there—for once! Then I'll tell you—if you care—more about it. Thanks awfully! Good-bye."

* * * * *

Later on, when "Miss Flink," in a state of sulky collapse, had been sent home in her taxi, Doris, Bentley, and Miss Wigram held a conference. But it came to little. Bentley, the hater of "rows," simply could not be moved to take the thing up. "I kept her from scalping him! —" he laughed—"and I'm not due for any more!" Doris said little. A whirl of arguments and projects were in her mind. But she kept her own counsel about them. As to the possibility of inducing the man to break it off, she repeated the only condition on which it could be done; at which Uncle Charles laughed, and Alice Wigram fell into a long and thoughtful silence.

* * * * *

Doris arrived at home rather early. What with the emotions of the day, the heat, and her work, she was strangely tired and over-done. After tea she strolled out into Kensington Gardens, and sat under the shade of trees already autumnal, watching the multitude of children—children of the people—enjoying the nation's park all to themselves, in the complete absence of their social betters. What ducks they were, some of them—the little, grimy, round-faced things—rolling on the grass, or toddling after their sisters and brothers. They turned large, inquisitive eyes upon her, which seemed to tease her heart-strings.

And suddenly, —it was in Kensington Gardens that out of the heart of a long and vague reverie there came a flash—an illumination—which wholly changed the life and future of Doris Meadows. After the thought in which it took shape had seized upon her, she sat for some time motionless; then rising to her feet, tottering a little, like one in bewilderment, she turned northwards, and made her way hurriedly towards Lancaster Gate. In a house there, lived a lady, a widowed lady, who was Doris's godmother, and to whom Doris—who had lost her own mother in her childhood—had turned for

A Great Success

counsel before now. How long it was since she had seen "Cousin Julia"! —nearly two months. And here she was, hastening to her, and not able to bear the thought that in all human probability Cousin Julia was not in town.

But, by good luck, Doris found her godmother, perching in London between a Devonshire visit and a Scotch one. They talked long, and Doris walked slowly home across the park. A glory of spreading sun lay over the grassy glades; the Serpentine held reflections of a sky barred with rose; London, transfigured, seemed a city of pearl and fire. And in Doris's heart there was a glory like that of the evening, —and, like the burning sky, bearing with it a promise of fair days to come. The glory and the promise stole through all her thoughts, softening and transmuting everything.

"When *he* grows up—if he were to marry such a woman—and I didn't know—if all *his* life—and mine—were spoilt—and nobody said a word!"

Her eyes filled with tears. She seemed to be walking with Arthur through a world of beauty, hand in hand.

How many hours to Pitlochry? She ran into the Kensington house, asking for railway guides, and peremptorily telling Jane to get down the small suitcase from the box-room at once.

PART III

CHAPTER V

"'Barbarians, Philistines, Populace!'"

The young golden-haired man of letters who was lounging on the grass beside Arthur Meadows repeated the words to himself in an absent voice, turning over the pages meanwhile of a book lying before him, as though in search of a passage he had noticed and lost. He presently found it again, and turned laughing towards Meadows, who was trifling with a French novel.

"Do you remember this passage in *Culture and Anarchy*—'I often, therefore, when I want to distinguish clearly the aristocratic class from the Philistines proper, or middle class, name the former, in my own mind, *the Barbarians*. And when I go through the country, and see this or that beautiful and imposing seat of theirs crowning the landscape, "There, " I say to myself, "is a great fortified post of the Barbarians! "'"

The youth pointed smiling to the fine Scotch house seen sideways on the other side of the lawn. Its turreted and battlemented front rose high above the low and spreading buildings which made the bulk of the house, so that it was a feudal castle—by no means, however, so old as it looked—on a front view, and a large and roomy villa from the rear. Meadows, looking at it, appreciated the fitness of the quotation, and laughed in response.

"Ungrateful wretch, " he said—"after that dinner last night! "

"All the same, Matthew Arnold had that dinner in mind—*chef* and all! Listen! 'The graver self of the Barbarian likes honours and consideration; his more relaxed self, field-sports and pleasures. ' Isn't it exact? Grouse-driving in the morning—bridge, politics, Cabinet-making, and the best of food in the evening. And I should put our hostess very high—wouldn't you? —among the chatelaines of the 'great fortified posts'? "

Meadows assented, but rather languidly. The day was extremely hot; he was tired, moreover, by a long walk with the guns the day before, and by conversation after dinner, led by Lady Dunstable, which had lasted up to nearly one o'clock in the morning. The talk had been brilliant, no doubt. Meadows, however, did not feel that he had come off very well in it. His hostess had deliberately pitted him against two of the ablest men in England, and he was well aware that he had disappointed her. Lady Dunstable had a way of behaving to her favourite author or artist of the moment as though she were the fancier and he the cock. She fought him against the other people's cocks with astonishing zeal and passion; and whenever he failed to kill, or lost too many feathers in the process, her annoyance was evident.

Meadows was in truth becoming a little tired of her dictation, although it was only ten days since he had arrived under her roof. There was a large amount of lethargy combined with his ability; and he hated to be obliged to live at any pace but his own. But Rachel Dunstable was an imperious friend, never tired herself, apparently, either in mind or body; and those who could not walk, eat, and talk to please her were apt to know it. Her opinions too, both political and literary, were in some directions extremely violent; and though, in general, argument and contradiction gave her pleasure, she had her days and moods, and Meadows had already suffered occasional sets-down, of a kind to which he was not accustomed.

But if he was—just a little—out of love with his new friend, in all other respects he was enjoying himself enormously. The long days on the moors, the luxurious life indoors, the changing and generally agreeable company, all the thousand easements and pleasures that wealth brings with it, the skilled service, the motors, the costly cigars, the wines—there was a Sybarite in Meadows which revelled in them all. He had done without them; he would do without them again; but there they were exceedingly good creatures of God, while they lasted; and only the hypocrites pretended otherwise. His sympathy, in the old poverty-stricken days, would have been all with the plaintive American—"There's d———-d good times in the world, and I ain't in 'em."

All the same, the fleshpots of Pitlochry had by no means put his wife out of his mind. His incurable laziness and procrastination in small things had led him to let slip post after post; but that very morning, at any rate, he had really written her a decent letter. And he was beginning to be anxious to hear from her about the yachting plan. If Lady Dunstable had asked him a few days later, he was not sure he would have accepted so readily. After all, the voyage might be stormy, and the lady—difficult. Doris must be dull in London, — "poor little cat!"

But then a very natural wrath returned upon him. Why on earth had she stayed behind? No doubt Lady Dunstable was formidable, but so was Doris in her own way. "She'd soon have held her own. Lady D. would have had to come to terms!" However, he remembered with some compunction that Doris did seem to have been a good deal neglected at Crosby Ledgers, and that he had not done much to help her.

*****

It was an "off" day for the shooters, and Lady Dunstable's guests were lounging about the garden, writing letters or playing a little leisurely golf on the lower reaches of the moor. Some of the ladies, indeed, had not yet appeared downstairs; a sleepy heat reigned over the valley with its winding stream, and veiled the distant hills. Meadows's companion, Ralph Barrow, a young novelist of promise, had gone fast asleep on the grass; Meadows was drowsing over his book; the dogs slept on the terrace steps; and in the summer silence the murmur of the river far below stole up the hill on which the house stood, and its soft song held the air.

Suddenly there was a disturbance. The dogs sprang up and barked. There was a firm step on the gravel. Lady Dunstable, stick in hand, her short leather-bound skirt showing boots and gaiters of the most business-like description, came quickly towards the seat on which Meadows sat.

"Mr. Meadows, I summon you for a walk! Sir Luke and Mr. Frome are coming. We propose to get to the tarn and back before lunch."

The tarn was at least two miles away, a stiff climb over difficult moor. Meadows, startled from something very near sleep, looked up, and a spirit of revolt seized upon him, provoked by the masterful tone and eyes of the lady.

"Very sorry, Lady Dunstable! —but I must write some letters before luncheon."

A Great Success

"Oh no!—put them off! I have been thinking of what you told me yesterday of your scheme for your new set of lectures. I have a great deal to say to you about it."

"I really shouldn't be worth talking to now," laughed Meadows; "this heat has made me so sleepy. To-night—or after tea—by all means!"

Lady Dunstable looked annoyed.

"I am expecting the Duke's party at tea," she said peremptorily. "This will be my only chance to-day."

"Then let's put it off—till to-morrow!" said Meadows, as he rose, still smiling. "It is most kind of you, but I really must write my letters, and my brains are pulp. But I will escort you through the garden, if I may."

His hostess turned sharply, and walked back towards the front of the house where Sir Luke and Mr. Frome, a young and rising Under-Secretary, were waiting for her. Meadows accompanied her, but found her exceedingly ungracious. She did, however, inform him, as they followed the other two towards the exit from the garden, that she had come to the conclusion that the subject he was proposing for his second series of lectures, to be given at Dunstable House during the winter, "would never do."

"Famous Controversies of the Nineteenth Century—political and religious." The very sound of it was enough to keep people away! "What people expect from you is talk about *persons*—not ideas. Ideas are not your line!"

Meadows flushed a little. What his "line" might be, he said, he had not yet discovered. But he liked his subject, and meant to stick to it.

Lady Dunstable turned on him a pair of sarcastic eyes.

"That's so like you clever people. You would die rather than take advice."

"Advice!—yes. As much as you like, dear lady. But—"

"But what—" she asked, imperatively, nettled in her turn.

"Well—you must put it prettily!" said Meadows, smiling. "We want a great deal of jam with the powder."

"You want to be flattered? I never flatter! It is the most despicable of arts."

"On the contrary—one of the most skilled. And I have heard you do it to perfection."

His daring half irritated, half amused her. It was her turn to flush. Her thin, sallow face and dark eyes lit up vindictively.

"One should never remind one's friends of their vices," she said with animation.

"Ah—if they *are* vices! But flattery is merely a virtue out of place—kindness gone wrong. From the point of view of the moralist, that is. From the point of view of the ordinary mortal, it is what no men—and few women—can do without!"

She smiled grimly, enjoying the spar. They carried it on a little while, Meadows, now fairly on his mettle, administering a little deft though veiled castigation here and there, in requital for various acts of rudeness of which she had been guilty towards him and others during the preceding days. She grew restive occasionally, but on the whole she bore it well. Her arrogance was not of the small-minded sort; and the best chance with her was to defy her.

At the gate leading on to the moor, Meadows resolutely came to a stop.

"Your letters are the merest excuse!" said Lady Dunstable. "I don't believe you will write one of them! I notice you always put off unpleasant duties."

"Give me credit at least for the intention."

Smiling, he held the gate open for her, and she passed through, discomfited, to join Sir Luke on the other side. Mr. Frome, the Under-Secretary, a young man of Jewish family and amazing talents, who had been listening with amusement to the conversation behind him, turned back to say to Meadows, at a safe distance—"Keep it up! —Keep it up! You avenge us all!"

A Great Success

* * * * *

Presently, as she and her two companions wound slowly up the moor, Sir Luke Malford, who had only arrived the night before, inquired gaily of his hostess:

"So she wouldn't come? —the little wife?"

"I gave her every chance. She scorned us."

"You mean—'she funked us.' Have you any idea, I wonder, how alarming you are?"

Lady Dunstable exclaimed impatiently:

"People represent me as a kind of ogre. I am nothing of the kind. I only expect everybody to play up."

"Ah, but you make the rules!" laughed Sir Luke. "I thought that young woman might have been a decided acquisition."

"She hadn't the very beginnings of a social gift," declared his companion. "A stubborn and rather stupid little person. I am much afraid she will stand in her husband's way."

"But suppose you blow up a happy home, by encouraging him to come without her? I bet anything she is feeling jealous and ill-used. You ought—I am sure you ought—to have a guilty conscience; but you look perfectly brazen!"

Sir Luke's banter was generally accepted with indifference, but on this occasion it provoked Lady Dunstable. She protested with vehemence that she had given Mrs. Meadows every chance, and that a young woman who was both trivial and conceited could not expect to get on in society. Sir Luke gathered from her tone that she and Mrs. Meadows had somewhat crossed swords, and that the wife might look out for consequences. He had been a witness of this kind of thing before in Lady Dunstable's circle; and he was conscious of a passing sympathy with the pleasant-faced little woman he remembered at Crosby Ledgers. At the same time he had been Rachel Dunstable's friend for twenty years; originally, her suitor. He spent a great part of his life in her company, and her ways seemed to him part of the order of things.

A Great Success

* * * * *

Meanwhile Meadows walked back to the house. He had been a good deal nettled by Lady Dunstable's last remark to him. But he had taken pains not to show it. Doris might say such things to him—but no one else. They were, of course, horribly true! Well—quarrelling with Lady Dunstable was amusing enough—when there was room to escape her. But how would it be in the close quarters of a yacht?

On his way through the garden he fell in with Miss Field—Mattie Field, the plump and smiling cousin of the house, who was apparently as necessary to the Dunstables in the Highlands, as in London, or at Crosby Ledgers. Her r'le in the Dunstable household seemed to Meadows to be that of "shock absorber. " She took all the small rubs and jars on her own shoulders, so that Lady Dunstable might escape them. If the fish did not arrive from Edinburgh, if the motor broke down, if a gun failed, or a guest set up influenza, it was always Miss Field who came to the rescue. She had devices for every emergency. It was generally supposed that she had no money, and that the Dunstables made her residence with them worth while. But if so, she had none of the ways of the poor relation. On the contrary, her independence was plain; she had a very free and merry tongue; and Lady Dunstable, who snubbed everybody, never snubbed Mattie Field. Lord Dunstable was clearly devoted to her.

She greeted Meadows rather absently.

"Rachel didn't carry you off? Oh, then—I wonder if I may ask you something? "

Meadows assured her she might ask him anything.

"I wonder if you will save yourself for a walk with Lord Dunstable. Will you ask him? He's very low, and you would cheer him up. "

Meadows looked at her interrogatively. He too had noticed that Lord Dunstable had seemed for some days to be out of spirits.

"Why do people have sons! " said Miss Field, briskly.

Meadows understood the reference. It was common knowledge among the Dunstables' friends that their son was anything but a comfort to them.

"Anything particularly wrong? " he asked her in a lowered voice, as they neared the house. At the same time, he could not help wondering whether, under all circumstances—if her nearest and dearest were made mincemeat in a railway accident, or crushed by an earth-quake—this fair-haired, rosy-cheeked lady would still keep her perennial smile. He had never yet seen her without it.

Miss Field replied in a joking tone that Lord Dunstable was depressed because the graceless Herbert had promised his parents a visit—a whole week—in August, and had now cried off on some excuse or other. Meadows inquired if Lady Dunstable minded as much as her husband.

"Quite! " laughed Miss Field. "It is not so much that she wants to see Herbert as that she's found someone to marry him to. You'll see the lady this afternoon. She comes with the Duke's party, to be looked at. "

"But I understand that the young man is by no means manageable? "

Miss Field's amusement increased.

"That's Rachel's delusion. She knows very well that she hasn't been able to manage him so far; but she's always full of fresh schemes for managing him. She thinks, if she could once marry him to the right wife, she and the wife between them could get the whip hand of him. "

"Does she care for him? " said Meadows, bluntly.

Miss Field considered the question, and for the first time Meadows perceived a grain of seriousness in her expression. But she emerged from her meditations, smiling as usual.

"She'd be hard hit if anything very bad happened! "

"What could happen? "

"Well, of course they never know whether he won't marry to please himself—produce somebody impossible! "

"And Lady Dunstable would suffer? "

Miss Field chuckled.

"I really believe you think her a kind of griffin—a stony creature with a hole where her heart ought to be. Most of her friends do. Rachel, of course, goes through life assuming that none of the disagreeable things that happen to other people will ever happen to her. But if they ever did happen—"

"The very stones would cry out? But hasn't she lost all influence with the youth?"

"She won't believe it. She's always scheming for him. And when he's not here she feels so affectionate and so good! And directly he comes—"

"I see! A tragedy—and a common one! Well, in half an hour I shall be ready for his lordship. Will you arrange it? I must write a letter first."

Miss Field nodded and departed. Meadows honestly meant to follow her into the house and write some pressing business letters. But the sunshine was so delightful, the sight of the empty bench and the abandoned novel on the other side of the lawn so beguiling, that after all he turned his lazy steps thither-ward, half ashamed, half amused to think how well Lady Dunstable had read his character.

The guests had all disappeared. Meadows had the garden to himself, and all its summer prospect of moor and stream. It was close on noon—a hot and heavenly day! And again he thought of Doris cooped up in London. Perhaps, after all, he would get out of that cruise!

Ah! there was the morning train—the midnight express from King's Cross just arriving in the busy little town lying in the valley at his feet. He watched it gliding along the valley, and heard the noise of the brakes. Were any new guests expected by it? he wondered. Hardly! The Lodge seemed quite full.

*****

Twenty minutes later he threw away the novel impatiently. Midway, the story had gone to pieces. He rose from his feet, intending this time to tackle his neglected duties in earnest. As he did so, he heard a motor climbing the steep drive, and in front of it a lady, walking.

He stood arrested—in a stupor of astonishment.

Doris!—by all the gods!—*Doris*!

It was indeed Doris. She came wearily, looking from side to side, like one uncertain of her way. Then she too perceived Meadows, and stopped.

Meadows was conscious of two mixed feelings—first, a very lively pleasure at the sight of her, and then annoyance. What on earth had she come for? To recover him?—to protest against his not writing?—to make a scene, in short? His guilty imagination in a flash showed her to him throwing herself into his arms—weeping—on this wide lawn—for all the world to see.

But she did nothing of the kind. She directed the motor, which was really a taxi from the station, to stop without approaching the front door, and then she herself walked quickly towards her husband.

"Arthur!—you got my letter? I could only write yesterday."

She had reached him, and they had joined hands mechanically.

"Letter?—I got no letter! If you posted one, it has probably arrived by your train. What on earth, Doris, is the meaning of this? Is there anything wrong?"

His expression was half angry, half concerned, for he saw plainly that she was tired and jaded. Of course! Long journeys always knocked her up. She meanwhile stood looking at him as though trying to read the impression produced on him by her escapade. Something evidently in his manner hurt her, for she withdrew her hand, and her face stiffened.

"There is nothing wrong with me, thank you! Of course I did not come without good reason."

"But, my dear, are you come to stay?" cried Meadows, looking helplessly at the taxi. "And you never wrote to Lady Dunstable?"

For he could only imagine that Doris had reconsidered her refusal of the invitation which had originally included them both, and—either tired of being left alone, or angry with him for not writing—had devised this *coup de main*, this violent shake to the kaleidoscope. But what an extraordinary step! It could only cover them both with ridicule. His cheeks were already burning.

Doris surveyed him very quietly.

"No—I didn't write to Lady Dunstable—I wrote to *you*—and sent her a message. I suppose—I shall have to stay the night."

"But what on earth are we to say to her?" cried Meadows in desperation. "They're out walking now—but she'll be back directly. There isn't a corner in the house! I've got a little bachelor room in the attics. Really, Doris, if you were going to do this, you should have given both her and me notice! There is a crowd of people here!"

Frown and voice were Jovian indeed. Doris, however, showed no tremors.

"Lady Dunstable will find somewhere to put me up," she said, half scornfully. "Is there a telegram for me?"

"A telegram? Why should there be a telegram? What is the meaning of all this? For heaven's sake, explain!"

Doris, however, did not attempt to explain. Her mood had been very soft on the journey. But Arthur's reception of her had suddenly stirred the root of bitterness again; and it was shooting fast and high. Whatever she had done or left undone, he ought *not* to have been able to conceal that he was glad to see her—he ought *not* to have been able to think of Lady Dunstable first! She began to take a pleasure in mystifying him.

"I expected a telegram. I daresay it will come soon. You see I've asked someone else to come this afternoon—and she'll have to be put up too."

"Asked someone else! —to Lady Dunstable's house!" Meadows stood bewildered. "Really, Doris, have you taken leave of your senses?"

A Great Success

She stood with shining eyes, apparently enjoying his astonishment. Then she suddenly bethought herself.

"I must go and pay the taxi." Turning round, she coolly surveyed the "fortified post." "It looks big enough to take me in. Arthur! —I think you may pay the man. Just take out my bag, and tell the footman to put it in your room. That will do for the present. I shall sit down here and wait for Lady Dunstable. I'm pretty tired."

The thought of what the magnificent gentleman presiding over Lady Dunstable's hall would say to the unexpected irruption of Mrs. Meadows, and Mrs. Meadows's bag, upon the "fortified post" he controlled, was simply beyond expressing. Meadows tried to face his wife with dignity.

"I think we'd better keep the taxi, Doris. Then you and I can go back to the hotel together. We can't force ourselves upon Lady Dunstable like this, my dear. I'd better go and tell someone to pack my things. But we must, of course, wait and see Lady Dunstable—though how you will explain your coming, and get yourself—and me—out of this absurd predicament, I cannot even pretend to imagine!"

Doris sat down—wearily.

"Don't keep the taxi, Arthur. I assure you Lady Dunstable will be very glad to keep both me—and my bag. Or if she won't—Lord Dunstable will."

Meadows came nearer—bent down to study her tired face.

"There's some mystery, of course, Doris, in all this! Aren't you going to tell me what it means?"

His wife's pale cheeks flushed.

"I would have told you—if you'd been the least bit glad to see me! But—if you don't pay the taxi, Arthur, it will run up like anything!"

She pointed peremptorily to the ticking vehicle and the impatient driver. Meadows went mechanically, paid the driver, shouldered the bag, and carried it into the hall of the Lodge. He then perceived that two grinning and evidently inquisitive footmen, waiting in the hall for anything that might turn up for them to do, had been watching

A Great Success

the whole scene—the arrival of the taxi, and the meeting between the unknown lady and himself, through a side window.

Burning to box someone's ears, Meadows loftily gave the bag to one of them with instructions that it should be taken to his room, and then turned to rejoin his wife.

As he crossed the gravel in front of the house, his mind ran through all possible hypotheses. But he was entirely without a clue—except the clue of jealousy. He could not hide from himself that Doris had been jealous of Lady Dunstable, and had perhaps been hurt by his rather too numerous incursions into the great world without her, his apparent readiness to desert her for cleverer women. "Little goose! —as if I ever cared twopence for any of them! "—he thought angrily. "And now she makes us both laughing-stocks! "

And yet, Doris being Doris—a proud, self-contained, well-bred little person, particularly sensitive to ridicule—the whole proceeding became the more incredible the more he faced it.

One o'clock! —striking from the church tower in the valley! He hurried towards the slight figure on the distant seat. Lady Dunstable might return at any moment. He foresaw the encounter—the great lady's insolence—Doris's humiliation—and his own. Well, at least let him agree with Doris on a common story, before his hostess arrived.

He sped across the grass, very conscious, as he approached the seat, of Doris's drooping look and attitude. Travelling all those hours! —and no doubt without any proper breakfast! However Lady Dunstable might behave, he would carry Doris into the Lodge directly, and have her properly looked after. Miss Field and he would see to that.

Suddenly—a sound of talk and laughter, from the shrubbery which divided the flower garden from the woods and the moor. Lady Dunstable emerged, with her two companions on either hand. Her vivid, masculine face was flushed with exercise and discussion. She seemed to be attacking the Under-Secretary, who, however, was clearly enjoying himself; while Sir Luke, walking a little apart, threw in an occasional gibe.

"I tell you your land policy here in Scotland will gain you nothing; and in England it will lose you everything. —Hullo! "

Lady Dunstable's exclamation, as she came to a stop and put up a tortoise-shell eyeglass, was clearly audible.

"Doris! " cried Meadows excitedly in his wife's ear—"Look here! — what are you going to say! —what am I to say! that you got tired of London, and wanted some Scotch air? —that we intend to go off together? —For goodness' sake, what is it to be? "

Doris rose, her lips breaking irrepressibly into smiles.

"Never mind, Arthur; I'll get through somehow. "

CHAPTER VI

The two ladies advanced towards each other across the lawn, while Meadows followed his wife in speechless confusion and annoyance, utterly at a loss how to extricate either himself or Doris; compelled, indeed, to leave it all to her. Sir Luke and the Under-Secretary had paused in the drive. Their looks as they watched Lady Dunstable's progress showed that they guessed at something dramatic in the little scene.

Nothing could apparently have been more unequal than the two chief actors in it. Lady Dunstable, with the battlements of "the great fortified post" rising behind her, tall and wiry of figure, her black hawk's eyes fixed upon her visitor, might have stood for all her class; for those too powerful and prosperous Barbarians who have ruled and enjoyed England so long. Doris, small and slight, in a blue cotton coat and skirt, dusty from long travelling, and a childish garden hat, came hesitatingly over the grass, with colour which came and went.

"How do you do, Mrs. Meadows! This is indeed an unexpected pleasure! I must quarrel with your husband for not giving us warning."

Doris's complexion had settled into a bright pink as she shook hands with Lady Dunstable. But she spoke quite composedly.

"My husband knew nothing about it, Lady Dunstable. My letter does not seem to have reached him."

"Ah? Our posts are very bad, no doubt; though generally, I must say, they arrive very punctually. Well, so you were tired of London? — you wanted to see how we were looking after your husband?"

Lady Dunstable threw a sarcastic glance at Meadows standing tongue-tied in the background.

"I wanted to see you," said Doris quietly, with a slight accent on the "you."

Lady Dunstable looked amused.

"Did you? How very nice of you! And you've—you've brought your luggage?" Lady Dunstable looked round her as though expecting to see it at the front door.

"I brought a bag. Arthur took it in for me."

"I'm so sorry! I assure you, if I had only known—But we haven't a corner! Mr. Meadows will bear me out—it's absurd, but true. These Scotch lodges have really no room in them at all!"

Lady Dunstable pointed with airy insolence to the spreading pile behind her. Doris—for all the agitation of her hidden purpose—could have laughed outright. But Meadows, rather roughly, intervened.

"We shall, of course, go to the hotel, Lady Dunstable. My wife's letter seems somehow to have missed me, but naturally we never dreamed of putting you out. Perhaps you will give us some lunch—my wife seems rather tired—and then we will take our departure."

Doris turned—put a hand on his arm—but addressed Lady Dunstable.

"Can I see you—alone—for a few minutes—before lunch?"

"*Before* lunch? We are all very hungry, I'm afraid," said Lady Dunstable, with a smile. Meadows was conscious of a rising fury. His quick sense perceived something delicately offensive in every word and look of the great lady. Doris, of course, had done an incredibly foolish thing. What she had come to say to Lady Dunstable he could not conceive; for the first explanation—that of a silly jealousy—had by now entirely failed him. But it was evident to him that Lady Dunstable assumed it—or chose to assume it. And for the first time he thought her odious!

Doris seemed to guess it, for she pressed his arm as though to keep him quiet.

"Before lunch, please," she repeated. "I think—you will soon understand." With an odd, and—for the first time—slightly puzzled look at her visitor, Lady Dunstable said with patronising politeness—

A Great Success

"By all means. Shall we come to my sitting-room?"

She led the way to the house. Meadows followed, till a sign from Doris waved him back. On the way Doris found herself greeted by Sir Luke Malford, bowed to by various unknown gentlemen, and her hand grasped by Miss Field.

"You do look done! Have you come straight from London? What—is Rachel carrying you off? I shall send you in a glass of wine and a biscuit directly!"

Doris said nothing. She got somehow through all the curious eyes turned upon her; she followed Lady Dunstable through the spacious passages of the Lodge, adorned with the usual sportsman's trophies, till she was ushered into a small sitting-room, Lady Dunstable's particular den, crowded with photographs of half the celebrities of the day—the poets, *savants*, and artists, of England, Europe, and America. On an easel stood a masterly small portrait of Lord Dunstable as a young man, by Bastien Lepage; and not far from it—rather pushed into a corner—a sketch by Millais of a fair-haired boy, leaning against a pony.

By this time Doris was quivering both with excitement and fatigue. She sank into a chair, and turned eagerly to the wine and biscuits with which Miss Field pursued her. While she ate and drank, Lady Dunstable sat in a high chair observing her, one long and pointed foot crossed over the other, her black eyes alive with satiric interrogation, to which, however, she gave no words.

The wine was reviving. Doris found her voice. As the door closed on Miss Field, she bent forward:—

"Lady Dunstable, I didn't come here on my own account, and had there been time of course I should have given you notice. I came entirely on your account, because something was happening to you—and Lord Dunstable—which you didn't know, and which made me—very sorry for you!"

Lady Dunstable started slightly.

"Happening to me?—and Lord Dunstable?"

"I have been seeing your son, Lady Dunstable."

An instant change passed over the countenance of that lady. It darkened, and the eyes became cold and wary.

"Indeed? I didn't know you were acquainted with him."

"I never saw him till a few days ago. Then I saw him—in my uncle's studio—with a woman—a woman to whom he is engaged."

Lady Dunstable started again.

"I think you must be mistaken," she said quickly, with a slight but haughty straightening of her shoulders.

Doris shook her head.

"No, I am not mistaken. I will tell you—if you don't mind—exactly what I have heard and seen."

And with a puckered brow and visible effort she entered on the story of the happenings of which she had been a witness in Bentley's studio. She was perfectly conscious—for a time—that she was telling it against a dead weight of half scornful, half angry incredulity on Lady Dunstable's part. Rachel Dunstable listened, indeed, attentively. But it was clear that she resented the story, which she did not believe; resented the telling of it, on her own ground, by this young woman whom she disliked; and resented above all the compulsory discussion which it involved, of her most intimate affairs, with a stranger and her social inferior. All sorts of suspicions, indeed, ran through her mind as to the motives that could have prompted Mrs. Meadows to hurry up to Scotland, without taking even the decently polite trouble to announce herself, bringing this unlikely and trumped-up tale. Most probably, a mean jealousy of her husband, and his greater social success! —a determination to force herself on people who had not paid the same attention to herself as to him, to *make* them pay attention, willy-nilly. Of course Herbert had undesirable acquaintances, and was content to go about with people entirely beneath him, in birth and education. Everybody knew it, alack! But he was really not such a fool—such a heartless fool—as this story implied! Mrs. Meadows had been taken in— willingly taken in—had exaggerated everything she said for her own purposes. The mother's wrath indeed was rapidly rising to the smiting point, when a change in the narrative arrested her.

"And then—I couldn't help it! "—there was a new note of agitation in Doris's voice—"but what had happened was so *horrid*—it was so like seeing a man going to ruin under one's eyes, for, of course, one knew that she would get hold of him again—that I ran out after your son and begged him to break with her, not to see her again, to take the opportunity, and be done with her! And then he told me quite calmly that he *must* marry her, that he could not help himself, but he would never live with her. He would marry her at a registry office, provide for her, and leave her. And then he said he would do it *at once*—that he was going to his lawyers to arrange everything as to money and so on—on condition that she never troubled him again. He was eager to get it done—that he might be delivered from her— from her company—which one could see had become dreadful to him. I implored him not to do such a thing—to pay any money rather than do it—but not to marry her! I begged him to think of you—and his father. But he said he was bound to her—he had compromised her, or some such thing; and he had given his word in writing. There was only one thing which could stop it—if she had told him lies about her former life. But he had no reason to think she had; and he was not going to try and find out. So then—I saw a ray of daylight—"

She stopped abruptly, looking full at the woman opposite, who was now following her every word—but like one seized against her will.

"Do you remember a Miss Wigram, Lady Dunstable—whose father had a living near Crosby Ledgers? "

Lady Dunstable moved involuntarily—her eyelids flickered a little.

"Certainly. Why do you ask? "

"*She* saw Mr. Dunstable—and Miss Flink—in my uncle's studio, and she was so distressed to think what—what Lord Dunstable"—there was a perceptible pause before the name—"would feel, if his son married her, that she determined to find out the truth about her. She told me she had one or two clues, and I sent her to a cousin of mine—a very clever solicitor—to be advised. That was yesterday morning. Then I got my uncle to find out your son—and bring him to me yesterday afternoon before I started. He came to our house in Kensington, and I told him I had come across some very doubtful stories about Miss Flink. He was very unwilling to hear anything.

After all, he said, he was not going to live with her. And she had nursed him—"

"Nursed him! " said Lady Dunstable, quickly. She had risen, and was leaning against the mantelpiece, looking sharply down upon her visitor.

"That was the beginning of it all. He was ill in the winter—in his lodgings. "

"I never heard of it! " For the first time, there was a touch of something natural and passionate in the voice.

Doris looked a little embarrassed.

"Your son told me it was pneumonia. "

"I never heard a word of it! And this—this creature nursed him? " The tone of the robbed lioness at last! —singularly inappropriate under all the circumstances. Doris struggled on.

"An actor friend of your son brought her to see him. And she really devoted herself to him. He declared to me he owed her a great deal—"

"He need have owed her nothing, " said Lady Dunstable, sternly. "He had only to send a postcard—a wire—to his own people. "

"He thought—you were so busy, " said Doris, dropping her eyes to the carpet.

A sound of contemptuous anger showed that her shaft—her mild shaft—had gone home. She hurried on—"But at last I got him to promise me to wait a week. That was yesterday at five o'clock. He wouldn't promise me to write to you—or his father. He seemed so desperately anxious to settle it all—in his own way. But I said a good deal about your name—and the family—and the horrible pain he would be giving—any way. Was it kind—was it right towards you, not only to give you *no* opportunity of helping or advising him—but also to take no steps to find out whether the woman he was going to marry was—not only unsuitable, wholly unsuitable—that, of course, he knows—but *a disgrace*? I argued with him that he must have some suspicion of the stories she has told him at different times, or he wouldn't have tried to protect himself in this particular way. He didn't deny it; but he said she had looked after him, and been kind to him, when nobody else was, and he should feel a beast if he pressed her too hardly."

"'When nobody else was'! " repeated Lady Dunstable, scornfully, her voice trembling with bitterness. "Really, Mrs. Meadows, it is very difficult for me to believe that my son ever used such words!"

Doris hesitated, then she raised her eyes, and with the happy feeling of one applying the scourge, in the name of Justice, she said with careful mildness: —

"I hope you will forgive me for telling you—but I feel as if I oughtn't to keep back anything—Mr. Dunstable said to me: 'My mother might have prevented it—but—she was never interested in me.'"

Another indignant exclamation from Lady Dunstable. Doris hurried on. "Only this is the important point! At last I got his promise, and I got it in writing. I have it here."

Dead silence. Doris opened her little handbag, took out a letter, in an open envelope, and handed it to Lady Dunstable, who at first seemed as if she were going to refuse it. However, after a moment's hesitation, she lifted her long-handled eyeglass and read it. It ran as follows:

DEAR MRS. MEADOWS, —I do not know whether I ought to do what you ask me. But you have asked me very kindly—you have really been awfully good to me, in taking so much trouble. I know I'm a stupid fool—they always told me so at home. But I don't want to do anything mean, or to go back on a woman who once did me a good turn; with whom also once—for I may as well be quite honest about it—I thought I was in love. However, I see there is something in what you say, and I will wait a week before marrying Miss Flink. But if you tell my people—I suppose you will—don't let them imagine they can break it off—except for that one reason. And *I* shan't lift a finger to break it off. I shall make no inquiries—I shall go on with the lawyers, and all that. My present intention is to marry Miss Flink—on the terms I have stated—in a week's time. If you do see my people—especially my father—tell them I'm awfully sorry to be such a nuisance to them. I got myself into the mess without meaning it, and now there's really only one way out. Thank you again.

A Great Success

Yours gratefully,
HERBERT DUNSTABLE.

Lady Dunstable crushed the letter in her hand. All pretence of incredulity was gone. She began to walk stormily up and down. Doris sank back in her chair, watching her, conscious of the most strangely mingled feelings, a touch of womanish triumph indeed, a pleasing sense of retribution, but, welling up through it, something profound and tender. If *he* should ever write such a letter to a stranger, while his mother was alive!

Lady Dunstable stopped.

"What chance is there of saving my son? " she said, peremptorily. "You will, of course, tell us all you know. Lord Dunstable must go to town at once. " She touched an electric bell beside her.

"Oh no! " cried Doris, springing up. "He mustn't go, please, until we have some more information. Miss Wigram is coming—this afternoon. "

Rachel Dunstable stood stupefied—with her hand on the bell.

"Miss Wigram—coming. "

"Don't you see? " cried Doris. "She was to spend all yesterday afternoon and evening in seeing two or three people—people who know. There is a friend of my uncle's—an artist—who saw a great deal of Miss Flink, and got to know a lot about her. Of course he may not have been willing to say anything, but I think he probably would—he was so mad with her for a trick she played him in the middle of a big piece of work. And if he was able to put us on any useful track, then Miss Wigram was to come up here straight, and tell you everything she could. But I thought there would have been a telegram—from her—" Her voice dropped on a note of disappointment.

There was a knock at the door. The butler entered, and at the same moment the luncheon gong echoed through the house.

"Tell Miss Field not to wait luncheon for me, " said Lady Dunstable sharply. "And, Ferris, I want his lordship's things packed at once, for London. Don't say anything to him at present, but in ten minutes' time just manage to tell him quietly that I should like to see him here. You understand—I don't want any fuss made. Tell Miss Field that Mrs. Meadows is too tired to come in to luncheon, and that I will come in presently."

The butler, who had the aspect of a don or a bishop, said "Yes, my lady," in that dry tone which implied that for twenty years the house of Dunstable had been built upon himself, as its rock, and he was not going to fail it now. He vanished, with just one lightning turn of the eyes towards the little lady in the blue linen dress; and Lady Dunstable resumed her walk, sunk in flushed meditation. She seemed to have forgotten Doris, when she heard an exclamation:—

"Ah, there *is* the telegram!"

And Doris, running to the window, waved to a diminutive telegraph boy, who, being new to his job, had come up to the front entrance of the Lodge instead of the back, and was now—recognising his misdeed—retreating in alarm from the mere aspect of "the great fortified post." He saw the lady at the window, however, and checked his course.

"For me!" cried Doris, triumphantly—and she tore it open.

Can't arrive till between eight and nine. Think I have got all we want. Please take a room for me at hotel. —ALICE WIGRAM.

Doris turned back into the room, and handed the telegram to Lady Dunstable, who read it slowly.

"Did you say this was the Alice Wigram I knew?"

"Her father had one of your livings," repeated Doris. "He died last year."

"I know. I quarrelled with him. I cannot conceive why Alice Wigram should do me a good turn!" Lady Dunstable threw back her head, her challenging look fixed upon her visitor. Doris was certain she had it in her mind to add—"or you either!"—but refrained.

"Lord Dunstable was always a friend to her father," said Doris, with the same slight emphasis on the "Lord" as before. "And she felt for the estate—the poor people—the tenants."

A Great Success

Rachel Dunstable shook her head impatiently.

"I daresay. But I got into a scrape with the Wigrams. I expect that you would think, Mrs. Meadows—perhaps most people would think, as of course her father did—that I once treated Miss Wigram unkindly!"

"Oh, what does it matter?" cried Doris, hastily, —"what *does* it matter? She wants to help—she's sorry for you. You should *see* that woman! It would be too awful if your son was tied to her for life!"

She sat up straight, all her soul in her eyes and in her pleasant face.

There was a pause. Then Lady Dunstable, whose expression had changed, came a little nearer to her.

"And you—I wonder why you took all this trouble?"

Doris said nothing. She fell back slowly in her chair, looking at the tall woman standing over her. Tears came into her eyes—brimmed—overflowed—in silence. Her lips smiled. Rachel Dunstable bent over her in bewilderment.

"To have a son," murmured Doris under her breath, "and then to see him ruined like this! No love for him! —no children—no grandchildren for oneself, when one is old—"

Her voice died away.

"'To have a son'?" repeated Lady Dunstable, wondering—"but you have none!"

Doris said nothing. Only she put up her hand feebly, and wiped away the tears—still smiling. After which she shut her eyes.

Lady Dunstable gasped. Then the long, sallow face flushed deeply. She walked over to a sofa on the other side of the room, arranged the pillows on it, and came back to Doris.

"Will you, please, let me put you on that sofa? You oughtn't to have had this long journey. Of course you will stay here—and Miss Wigram too. It seems—I shall owe you a great deal—and I could not have expected you—to think about me—at all. I can do rude things. But I can also—be sorry for my sins! "

Doris heard an awkward and rather tremulous laugh. Upon which she opened her eyes, no less embarrassed than her hostess, and did as she was told. Lady Dunstable made her as comfortable as a hand so little used to the feminine arts could manage.

"Now I will send you in some luncheon, and go and talk to Lord Dunstable. Please rest till I come back. "

* * * * *

Doris lay still. She wanted very much to see Arthur, and she wondered, till her head ached, whether he would think her a great fool for her pains. Surely he would come and find her soon. Oh, the time people spent on lunching in these big houses!

The vibration of the train seemed to be still running through her limbs. She was indeed wearied out, and in a few minutes, what with the sudden quiet and the softness of the cushions which had been spread for her, she fell unexpectedly asleep.

When she woke, she saw her husband sitting beside her—patiently—with a tray on his knee.

"Oh, Arthur! —what time is it? Have I been asleep long? "

"Nearly an hour. I looked in before, but Lady Dunstable wouldn't let me wake you. She—and he—and I—have been talking. Upon my word, Doris, you've been and gone and done it! But don't say anything! You've got to eat this chicken first. "

He fed her with it, looking at her the while with affectionate and admiring eyes. Somehow, Doris became dimly aware that she was going to be a heroine.

"Have they told you, Arthur? "

"Everything that you've told her. (No—not everything! —thought Doris.) You *are* a brick, Doris! And the way you've done it! That's what impresses her ladyship! She knows very well that she would have muffed it. You're the practical woman! Well, you can rest on your laurels, darling! You'll have the whole place at your feet—beginning with your husband—who's been dreadfully bored without you. There!"

He put down his Jovian head, and rubbed his cheek tenderly against hers, till she turned round, and gave him the lightest of kisses.

"Was he an abominable correspondent?" he said, repentantly.

"Abominable!"

"Did you hate him!"

"Whenever I had time. When do you start on your cruise, Arthur!"

"Any time—some time—never!" he said, gaily. "Give me that Capel Curig address, and I'll wire for the rooms this afternoon. I came to the conclusion this morning that the same yacht couldn't hold her ladyship and me."

"Oh!—so she's been chastening *you*?" said Doris, well pleased.

Meadows nodded.

"The rod has not been spared—since Sunday. It was then she got tired of me. I mark the day, you see, almost the hour. My goodness! —if you're not always up to your form—epigrams, quotations—all pat—"

"She plucks you—without mercy. Down you slither into the second class!" Doris's look sparkled.

"There you go—rejoicing in my humiliations!" said Meadows, putting an arm round the scoffer. "I tell you, she proposes to write my next set of lectures for me. She gave me an outline of them this morning."

Then they both laughed together like children. And Doris, with her head on a strong man's shoulder, and a rough coat scrubbing her cheek, suddenly bethought her of the line—"Journeys end in lovers' meeting—" and was smitten with a secret wonder as to how much of her impulse to come north had been due to an altruistic concern for the Dunstable affairs, and how much to a firm determination to recapture Arthur from his Gloriana. But that doubt she would never reveal. It would be so bad for Arthur!

She rose to her feet.

"Where are they?"

"Lord and Lady Dunstable? Gone off to Dunkeld to find their solicitor and bring him back to meet Miss Wigram. They'll be home by tea. I'm to look after you."

"Are we going to an hotel?"

Meadows laughed immoderately.

"Come and look at your apartment, my dear. One of her ladyship's maids has been told off to look after you. As I expect you have arrived with little more than a comb-and-brush bag, there will be a good deal to do."

Doris caught him by the coat-fronts.

"You don't mean to say that I shall be expected to dine to-night! I have *not* brought an evening dress."

"What does that matter? I met Miss Field in the passage, as I was coming in to you, and she said: 'I see Mrs. Meadows has not brought much luggage. We can lend her anything she wants. I will send her a few of Rachel's tea-gowns to choose from.'"

Doris's laugh was hysterical; then she sobered down.

"What time is it? Four o'clock. Oh, I wish Miss Wigram was here! You know, Lord Dunstable must go to town to-night! And Miss Wigram can't arrive till after the last train from here."

"They know. They've ordered a special, to take Lord Dunstable and the solicitor to Edinburgh, to catch the midnight mail."

"Oh, well—if you can bully the fates like that! —" said Doris, with a shrug. "How did he take it?"

Meadows's tone changed.

A Great Success

"It was a great blow. I thought it aged him."

"Was she nice to him?" asked Doris, anxiously.

"Nicer than I thought she could be," said Meadows, quietly. "I heard her say to him—'I'm afraid it's been my fault, Harry.' And he took her hand, without a word."

"I will *not* cry!" said Doris, pressing her hands on her eyes. "If it comes right, it will do them such a world of good! Now show me my room."

But in the hall, waiting to waylay them, they found Miss Field, beaming as usual.

"Everything is ready for you, dear Mrs. Meadows, and if you want anything you have only to ring. This way—"

"The ground-floor?" said Doris, rather mystified, as they followed.

"We have put you in what we call—for fun—our state-rooms. Various Royalties had them last year. They're in a special wing. We keep them for emergencies. And the fact is we haven't got another corner."

Doris, in dismay, took the smiling lady by the arm.

"I can't live up to it! Please let us go to the inn."

But Meadows and Miss Field mocked at her; and she was soon ushered into a vast bedroom, in the midst of which, on a Persian carpet, sat her diminutive bag, now empty. Various elegant "confections" in the shape of tea-gowns and dressing-gowns littered the bed and the chairs. The toilet-table showed an array of coroneted brushes. As for the superb Empire bed, which had belonged to Queen Hortense, and was still hung with the original blue velvet sprinkled with golden bees, Doris eyed it with a firm hostility.

"We needn't sleep in it," she whispered in Meadows's ear. "There are two sofas."

Meanwhile Miss Field and others flitted about, adding all the luxuries of daily use to the splendour of the rooms. Gardeners appeared bringing in flowers, and an anxious maid, on behalf of her ladyship, begged that Mrs. Meadows would change her travelling dress for a comfortable white tea-gown, before tea-time, suggesting another "creation" in black and silver for dinner. Doris, frowning and reluctant, would have refused; but Miss Field said softly "Won't you? Rachel will be so distressed if she mayn't do these little things for you. Of course she doesn't deserve it; but—"

"Oh yes—I'll put them on—if she likes, " said Doris, hurriedly. "It doesn't matter. "

Miss Field laughed. "I don't know where all these things come from, " she said, looking at the array. "Rachel buys half of them for her maids, I should think—she never wears them. Well, now I shall leave you till tea-time. Tea will be on the lawn—Mr. Meadows knows where. By the way—" she looked, smiling, at Meadows—"they've put off the Duke. If you only knew what that means. "

She named a great Scotch name, the chief of the ancient house to which Lady Dunstable belonged. Miss Field described how this prince of Dukes paid a solemn visit every year to Franick Castle, and the eager solicitude—almost agitation—with which the visit was awaited, by Lady Dunstable in particular.

"You don't mean, " cried Doris, "that there is anybody in the whole world who frightens Lady Dunstable? "

"As she frightens us? Yes! —on this one day of the year we are all avenged. Rachel, metaphorically, sits on a stool and tries to please. To put off 'the Duke' by telephone! —what a horrid indignity! But I've just inflicted it. "

Mattie Field smiled, and was just going away when she was arrested by a timid question from Doris.

"Please—shall Arthur go down to Pitlochry and engage a room for Miss Wigram? "

Miss Field turned in amusement.

"A room! Why, it's all ready! She is your lady-in-waiting. "

A Great Success

And taking Doris by the arm she led her to inspect a spacious apartment on the other side of a passage, where the Lady Alice or Lady Mary without whom Royal Highnesses do not move about the world was generally put up.

"I feel like Christopher Sly, " said Doris, surveying the scene, with her hands in her jacket pockets. "So will she. But never mind! "

* * * * *

Events flowed on. Lord and Lady Dunstable came back by tea-time, bringing with them the solicitor, who was also the chief factor of their Scotch estate. Lord Dunstable looked old and wearied. He came to find Doris on the lawn, pressing her hand with murmured words of thanks.

"If that child Alice Wigram—of course I remember her well! —brings us information we can go upon, we shall be all right. At least there's hope. My poor boy! Anyway, we can never be grateful enough to you. "

As for Lady Dunstable, the large circle which gathered for tea under a group of Scotch firs talked indeed, since Franick Castle existed for that purpose, but they talked without a leader. Their hostess sat silent and sombre, with thoughts evidently far away. She took no notice of Meadows whatever, and his attempts to draw her fell flat. A neighbour had walked over, bringing with him—maliciously—a Radical M. P. whose views on the Scotch land question would normally have struck fire and fury from Lady Dunstable. She scarcely recognised his name, and he and the Under-Secretary launched into the most despicable land heresies under her very nose—unrebuked. She had not an epigram to throw at anyone. But her eyes never failed to know where Doris Meadows was, and indeed, though no one but the two or three initiated knew why, Doris was in some mysterious but accepted way the centre of the party. Everybody spoiled her; everybody smiled upon her. The white tea-gown which she wore—miracle of delicate embroidery— had never suited Lady Dunstable; it suited Doris to perfection. Under her own simple hat, her eyes—and they were very fine eyes— shone with a soft and dancing humour. It was all absurd—her being there—her dress—this tongue-tied hostess—and these agreeable men who made much of her! She must get Arthur out of it as soon as possible, and they would look back upon it and laugh. But for the moment it was pleasant, it was stimulating! She found herself arguing about the new novels, and standing at bay against a whole group of clever folk who were tearing Mr. Augustus John and other gods of her idolatry to pieces. She was not shy; she never really had been; and to find that she could talk as well as other people—or most other people—even in these critical circles, excited her. The circle round her grew; and Meadows, standing on the edge of it, watched her with astonished eyes.

* * * * *

The northern evening sank into a long and glowing twilight. The hills stood in purple against a tawny west, and the smoke from the little town in the valley rose clear and blue into air already autumnal. The guests of Franick had scattered in twos and threes over the gardens and the moor, while Doris, her host and hostess, and the solicitor, sat and waited for Alice Wigram. She came with the evening train, tired, dusty, and triumphant; and the information she brought with her was more than enough to go upon. The past of Elena Flink—poor lady!—shone luridly out; and even the countenance of the solicitor cleared. As for Lord Dunstable, he grasped the girl by both hands.

"My dear child, what you have done for us! Ah, if your father were here!"

And bending over her, with the courtly grace of an old man, he kissed her on the brow. Alice Wigram flushed, turning involuntarily towards Lady Dunstable.

"Rachel!—don't we owe her everything," said Lord Dunstable with emotion—"her and Mrs. Meadows? But for them, our boy might have wrecked his life."

"He appears to have been a most extraordinary fool!" said Lady Dunstable with energy: —a recrudescence of the natural woman, which was positively welcome to everybody. And it did not prevent the passage of some embarrassed but satisfactory words between Herbert Dunstable's mother and Alice Wigram, after Lady Dunstable had taken her latest guest to "Lady Mary's" room, bidding her go straight to bed, and be waited on.

Lord Dunstable and the lawyer departed after dinner to meet their special train at Perth. Lady Dunstable, with variable spirits, kept the evening going, sometimes in a brown study, sometimes as brilliant and pugnacious as ever. Doris slipped out of the drawing-room once or twice to go and gossip with Alice Wigram, who was lying under silken coverings, inclined to gentle moralising on the splendours of the great, and much petted by Miss Field and the house-keeper.

"How nice you look! " said the girl shyly, on one occasion, as Doris came stealing in to her. "I never saw such a pretty gown! "

"Not bad! " said Doris complacently, throwing a glance at the large mirror near. It was still the white tea-gown, for she had firmly declined to sample anything else, in truth well aware that Arthur's eyes approved both it and her in it.

"Lord Dunstable has been so kind, " whispered Miss Wigram. "He said I must always henceforth look upon him as a kind of guardian. Of course I should never let him give me a farthing! "

"Why no, that's the kind of thing one couldn't do! " said Doris with decision. "But there are plenty of other ways of being nice. Well—here we all are, as happy as larks; and what we've really done, I suppose, is to take a woman's character away, and give her another push to perdition. "

"She hadn't any character! " cried Alice Wigram indignantly. "And she would have gone to perdition without us, and taken that poor youth with her. Oh, I know, I know! But morals are a great puzzle to me. However, I firmly remind myself of that 'one in the eye, ' and then all my doubts depart. Good-night. Sleep well! You know very well that I should have shirked it if it hadn't been for you! "

* * * * *

A little later the Meadowses stood together at the open window of their room, which led by a short flight of steps to a flowering garden below. All Franick had gone to bed, and this wing in which the "state-rooms" were, seemed to be remote from the rest of the house. They were alone; the night was balmy; and there was a flood of secret joy in Doris's veins which gave her a charm, a beguilement Arthur had never seen in her before. She was more woman, and therefore more divine! He could hardly recall her as the careful housewife, harassed by lack of pence, knitting her brows over her butcher's books, mending endless socks, and trying to keep the nose of a lazy husband to the grindstone. All that seemed to have vanished. This white sylph was pure romance—pure joy. He saw her anew; he loved her anew.

"Why did you look so pretty to-night? You little witch! " he murmured in her ear, as he held her close to him.

"Arthur! "—she drew herself away from him. "*Did* I look pretty? Honour bright! "

"Delicious! How often am I to say it? "

"You'd better not. Don't wake the devil in me, Arthur! It's all this tea-gown. If you go on like this, I shall have to buy one like it. "

"Buy a dozen! " he said joyously. "Look there, Doris—you see that path? Let's go on to the moor a little. "

Out they crept, like truant children, through the wood-path and out upon the moor. Meadows had brought a shawl, and spread it on a rock, full under the moonlight. There they sat, close together, feeling all the goodness and glory of the night, drinking in the scents of heather and fern, the sounds of plashing water and gently moving winds. Above them, the vault of heaven and the friendly stars; below them, the great hollow of the valley, the scattered lights, the sounds of distant trains.

"She didn't kiss me when she said good-night! " said Doris suddenly. "She wasn't the least sentimental—or ashamed—or grateful! Having said what was necessary, she let it alone. She's a real lady—though rather a savage. I like her! "

"Who are you talking of? Lady Dunstable? I had forgotten all about her. All the same, darling, I should like to know what made you do all this for a woman you *said* you detested! "

"I did detest her. I shall probably detest her again. Leopards don't change their spots, do they? But I shan't—fear her any more! "

Something in her tone arrested Meadows's attention.

A Great Success

"What do you mean?"

"Oh, what I say!" cried Doris, drawing herself a little from him, with a hand on his shoulder. "I shall never fear her, or anyone, any more. I'm safe! Why did I do it? Do you really want to know? I did it—because—I was so sorry for her—poor silly woman,—who can't get on with her own son! Arthur! —if our son doesn't love me better than hers loves her—you may kill me, dear, and welcome!"

"Doris! There is something in your voice—! What are you hiding from me?"

* * * * *

But as to the rest of that conversation under the moon, let those imagine it who may have followed this story with sympathy.

THE END

Copyright © 2021 Esprios Digital Publishing. All Rights Reserved.

Lightning Source UK Ltd.
Milton Keynes UK
UKHW040631030921
389968UK00001B/185